STRANGER A[...]

Be[...]don
th[...]y to
ge[...]sive
po[...]She
so[...]of
ha[...]age
ca[...]on
he[...]fate
m[...]me
so[...]han
wa[...]wly
en[...]ing
co[...]self
qu[...]uld
sh[...]

STRANGER AT THE DOOR

Faith Alexander

Curley Publishing, Inc.
South Yarmouth, Ma.

Library of Congress Cataloging-in-Publication Data

Alexander, Faith.
  Stranger at the door / Faith Alexander.
    p.   cm.
  Originally published: London: Robert Hale, 1990.
  ISBN 0–7927–0909–8 (hard: large print).—
  ISBN 0–7927–0910–1 (soft: large print).
  1. Large type books. I. Title.
  [PR6051.L3557S77 1992]   91–24197
  823′.914—dc20   CIP

Published in Large Print by arrangement with Robert Hale Limited.

Printed in Great Britain

This book is affectionately dedicated to Alison,
and Joseph John.

STRANGER AT THE DOOR

CHAPTER ONE

Bethan Blake gently placed a slim hand over her wine-glass, declining any more. She smiled at Harvey Lime, who was always lavish with his entertaining. He liked to be seen in the best clubs and restaurants, the best theatre seats, although a lot of that came free with his job as a top show business agent. Harvey knew the value of being in the right place, being seen with the right people.

Tonight it was The Talkabout, a night-spot that cropped up frequently in the gossip columns. Bethan had a headache, a nasty little niggle that promised to grow worse. The meal, like so many others, had been good, the atmosphere sophisticated, but she had a sudden sharp longing for the solitude of her own flat. For space. For freedom.

However, it would be the early hours before she could get away. At this moment, London's swinging nightlife seemed gaudy and superficial. What was she dreaming about? Harvey wanted her here, so that was that. At twenty-five, she had been his personal assistant for two years. Jobs like hers were rarer than rubies, the envy of many.

He leaned across the table, a paunchy man of nearly fifty, in a suit a shade too young, the

1

clamour of his life now firmly etched in the greyness of his face.

'It won't be long now.'

He cocked an eye towards the area designated for the cabaret. In the background, a pianist had been playing jazz, but the main attraction was still to come.

'Let's hope he's on form.'

Harvey started to pour himself another glass, then changed his mind. He's nervous, thought Bethan, with a twinge of understanding. Handling popular singers took a great deal of know-how, and Trash Morgan was one of Harvey's 'names'.

Sympathy for Harvey and dark resentment of Morgan warred in Bethan's brain. She hadn't wanted to come, Harvey knew her feelings, but his maxim was never mix business and personal dislikes.

He pushed the glass aside.

'You look stunning,' he said.

'Thank you,' she murmured, no less sincere because Harvey had an automatic line in such chat. The shining fair hair, the brilliant blue dress that caught the blue of her eyes, the enormous ear-rings that emphasised her high cheek-bones—Bethan knew that her looks had helped her to get and keep her job. So she must expect to be trotted around as part of his circus.

'You've got to come,' he had insisted about tonight. 'I don't give a damn what you think of

Morgan. You know he likes women. And he needs all the back-up he can get, because—'

Harvey had sunk into silence, but he didn't have to spell it out to Bethan. She knew Morgan's career was shaky. He wasn't the top liner he had been. He was difficult, unpredictable, and harshly uncompromising about the engagements he took. Tonight was just a sprat to catch a mackerel.

The lights were dimming, changing. The room blacked, then the stab of a spotlight picked out a lean figure in white, strung like a bow against the microphone; white open-necked shirt, white trews, white sandals, a thin face, and a riot of red curling hair.

He looks like a match about to be struck, thought Bethan cruelly. And not a bad analogy at that, because he exuded charisma, the vitality of a man about to catch fire. She couldn't see him, or hear him, ever, without a twist of hatred. She was glad of the darkness that helped to hide her face.

The room had quietened, tribute to his haunting voice, notes that pulled at the heart-strings, sent shivers of pleasure tingling over the skin. She sensed rather than saw Harvey sit back and relax. This was one of Trash Morgan's better nights. He had the audience with him. Even the sound of chinking glasses had died away.

His voice was strangely timeless, light and yet

penetrating, although Bethan knew he could launch himself into harsh, raucous songs of rebellion when his mood dictated.

A song finished, applause flared, and he picked up a guitar. From the first chord, she knew what was coming next. No, no. She ground the words savagely together under her breath. Not that one—a song of young love, and bright dreams.

He had sung that one on the night she had taken her young sister Alys along as part of a crowd to hear Trash Morgan, to meet him.

Did he *know* that Bethan Blake was here with Harvey Lime tonight? That Alys Blake's sister was listening to his throbbing words? Of course he knew. Hot anger seared through Bethan's blood. Was he so insensitive that he didn't recall Alys Blake? Did he go through so many women that he didn't remember one bright butterfly that had bruised her wings against him?

It was one of the songs that had made him, and Bethan knew that she would never hear it for the rest of her life without seeing Alys's face, ravaged with weeping. Because she had fallen for his magnetism, his music, and he had marked her life indelibly.

I hate him, thought Bethan, hard as diamonds. I hate him for Alys, and her despair. Why should he make a shambles of other people's lives, and just move on? If his career ended tomorrow, Bethan wouldn't give a brass farthing.

But he was going down well here tonight, and Harvey would be pleased, because Morgan's career badly needed a lift, and there was the prospect of a part in an American musical, although Harvey was having a struggle to get it.

She couldn't sit here, washed in his melancholy music, as he cast a web over his listeners. Bethan leaned over and touched Harvey's hand.

'I'm going to the powder-room.'

'Okay, okay. Don't be long.' He was preoccupied, and Bethan suddenly registered that he didn't look well. 'You know we're meeting people. If Morgan just keeps his cool—'

She spun out her reprieve as long as she could. Later would come the noise, the gossip, the insincere remarks, the patched-over lies and half-promises.

I'm tired, she told herself, looking in the mirror at the dark shadows under her eyes. Tonight it all seemed shallow and superficial. Where was sunlight? Where was bright hope and sincerity?

She returned to her table just before the lights went up, then people were on their feet applauding. Girls surged forward, pressing around the singer. Harvey started to move.

'We're going on to the hotel where the

Americans are staying. Do your best. Morgan needs this break.'

Does he? thought Bethan. What about Alys? What did she need?

The party was a big one, swelled by people Bethan recognised as the inevitable hangers-on. Time passed before Morgan put in an appearance. Harvey guided him to the right places and the right people, whilst Bethan painted on a smile.

It was two a.m. before she was able to call a taxi, and get away to her flat in a fashionable suburb. Harvey was still at the party, his collar loose, his face tinged with a clayish hue. In spite of his brash hardness, he was a family man, with a wife who shunned the bright lights, so she must see very little of him. There were two grown-up sons.

Bethan yearned for sleep, but it was a long time coming. She couldn't get Alys out of her mind, although she told herself over and over again that there was no point in raking over dead ashes; that Alys was all right, thousands of miles away, working in Vancouver. Alys had come through, sadder if not wiser, though she was still only nineteen.

I miss her, thought Bethan, lonely in the small hours, when everything seemed worse. She finally dozed, but was up in time to be at the office by ten, finding Harvey there before her. He looked washed-out but confident, and

6

she knew he was pleased about last night. Things had gone well, the offer had been made, and Morgan was to sign the contract this afternoon.

Other matters occupied Bethan until after a sandwich lunch. Harvey came back in just before three, bristling with the subdued nervous tension she knew so well. The American representative and his side-kick were due in ten minutes.

Bethan sent the office junior to prepare coffee, and kept her face impassive.

'Where *is* he?' fumed Harvey. 'In heaven's name—can't he tell the time?'

'Didn't you arrange to pick him up?'

'He wouldn't have it. You know how difficult he can be—likes to think he's a loner.'

And that's not all, thought Bethan cynically.

'Probably hung-over,' she said, then regretted it, for whatever he was, Trash Morgan was not a drinker.

The Americans arrived, sprawling easily in the leather chairs. Although they didn't say so, Bethan knew they expected Morgan to be there waiting. Easy conversation started to drag. After half an hour, and several phone calls, there was still no sign of the singer.

The Americans had a schedule to keep to, and Morgan was only a small part of it. When they had gone, Bethan sought for words to restore Harvey's composure. He was a man who

7

could occasionally bluster, but she had never seen him so angry.

'He's blown it. They're not gonna hang about—why should they? If he doesn't sign, and soon, he's out.'

Bethan had to hand it to Harvey, he calmed down pretty quickly, told her to take the rest of the afternoon off, and said he intended to go tracking down Morgan. She nodded, grateful for the prospect of a quiet evening, and went home to write to Alys.

The four walls of her flat were old friends. Like Morgan, she didn't mind being alone, although Bethan had often thought that he only assumed this enigmatic role to impress his public.

Tonight she had no regrets about her lack of a husband or lover. A long-term relationship had broken up around the time of Alys's trouble. It had seemed that both of them were fated to be unlucky with men.

Sleep claimed her, but the telephone woke her a good hour before she need get up. Yawning, Bethan reached for the receiver. Immediately an excited voice spilled out a torrent of words.

'Bethan? Oh, I'm glad I caught you before you left. It's about Harvey. He told me to get hold of you, and—'

'Mary, what's wrong?' Shades of sleep vanished.

'He had a bump in his car last night, pretty bad. This van came out of a side-road, straight into him. His car's a write-off. It's a miracle he wasn't more badly hurt. I'm just grateful for that.'

Mary Lime's voice was shaking, and Bethan suspected that she was crying.

'Where is he?' she asked quietly.

'St. Stephen's infirmary. I got on the phone to Mark, and he came round. He's a good son, one of the best. We were there with Harvey until after midnight. Harvey says—'

Sympathetically, Bethan untangled the story. Harvey wanted her to go to the hospital as soon as she could. It was run on modern lines, so there was no problem about visiting.

She showered and dressed, then after a light breakfast took a taxi to St. Stephen's. Reception directed her to the floor where Harvey was a patient. He was sitting disconsolately propped up against a mound of pillows. Although he appeared subdued, he didn't look nearly so bad as Bethan had expected. With a few brief words he dismissed his troubles; cuts, bruises, a whiplash injury to the neck, no break, although bones in his left hand were broken.

'Harvey—what rotten luck.' Tears brimmed up in Bethan's eyes. To her relief, he grinned.

'They're not keeping me here more than a day or two. No chance. What I want you to do is get off after Morgan. He's run back to his

9

bolthole. Playing the hermit again, while he sorts out his head.'

'So what do I do?'

'Pick up the papers in the office—deal with anything urgent, and tell the girl to stall everything else. Then head for Lincolnshire!'

'And how will I find this village?'

'Southbeck won't be signposted until you're about ten miles away. I'll jot you down some road numbers.'

Harvey's sister Maggie owned a weekend cottage in a rural village, and early in their association Harvey had taken Morgan there, pandering to his spiel about the simple life and living with nature. At that time, the singer's earnings had been high. He had bought a nearby farm, and fled there whenever he wished to go to ground.

'It may not be easy,' said Bethan guardedly.

'Stay till you nail him. Stay at Maggie's place. The keys are at the inn. And stick to Morgan like a leech. He's washed up if he lets this go.'

She left Harvey, knowing from experience that the bed wouldn't hold him long. Back at the office it took an hour to sort things out, then Bethan returned to her flat where she put a few essentials in her case. The caretaker for the building brought her car round for her.

It was a smart yet practical model, frequently advertised on television, and it gave her pleasure to drive it. Before lunch-time she was on the road.

Once she was clear of London the miles fell away. The countryside opened up in front of her, with rolling fields like prairies stretching to the horizon. The sky was clearer, the air kinder. June sunshine fell kindly on flourishing crops. Here and there were bright acres of flowers, row upon row .

Bethan wound the window down, letting the wind tangle her hair. In some way she couldn't explain, she had shed a skin, felt easier, lighter. The hassle of her job, the tempo of a life that was geared to shifting values, greed, and surface glamour—these receded.

On the back seat lay a black leather document-case, inside it the papers for signing. What do I care about Morgan's career, thought Bethan? What had *he* cared for Alys? Morgan needs the break, Harvey had said.

If the man is such a fool that he walks out on an offer, thought Bethan, with clear, cold malice, why should *anybody* give a damn?

The Americans wouldn't wait long, and there were other singers falling over each other for the chance. The matter had fallen into Bethan's hands, a development she could not have foreseen. Maybe fate was giving her a chance to even the balance. If Morgan didn't sign, he didn't work.

It shouldn't be so hard not to find Morgan. He was, after all, notorious for his

11

disappearing-acts. Why should he expect a successful career if he wasn't prepared to follow it heart and soul?

Bethan had just noticed the first signpost for the village. Ten minutes later she drove into Southbeck, collected the key from the inn, and went to find Maggie's cottage.

CHAPTER TWO

Leaving the main street, as instructed at the inn, she took a lane between neat hedges and creamy banks of hawthorn blossom. A row of three cottages stood set back, then just past these a pleasant, pantiled dwelling with a walled garden. Bethan parked the car and got out.

Her arrival did not go un-noticed. A woman emerged from the middle cottage and started to clean the windows. Bethan paused, looking at the label on the key in her hand. The woman turned, and waved her wash-leather.

'Can I help you?' she called.

'Er—it's quite all right, thank you.'

Smiling a little, Bethan went inside. The front door opened straight into a large room with an open fireplace, polished wooden floors, and cheerful rugs. A basket of logs stood on the hearth. Beyond this room lay a neat and tidy kitchen, with stainless steel units, and modern fittings. Its wide window looked onto the garden, which was bursting into the full joy of bloom and colour.

It was a pleasant place, and Bethan felt a lift of the spirit. She climbed the open staircase to the bedrooms above. Wide window-sills told of thick walls, and attractive rooms trapped the afternoon sunlight.

She chose her bedroom at the back of the house, opened the windows, and stood listening to the birds. Long hours stretched in front of her. She could of course go in search of Morgan. Maybe she would. Maybe.

She changed into casual clothes, and fixed a simple meal from the food she had brought. A curious feeling possessed Bethan, a mixture of rebellion and relief.

Harvey knew how much she disliked Morgan, but he had sent her here to nail him. Who would be any the wiser if she just kicked her heels for a couple of days?

Because she had slipped the net—if only for a while, with very little to remind her of the doubts in her life. The air outside was too good to miss. Bethan locked the cottage door and set off to look round the village.

It didn't take long. A grey Saxon church dominated the small houses huddled near it, looking onto a green. There was one street, with the usual small shops and a post-office. The more expensive houses, the homes of commuters and weekend visitors, lay on the outskirts.

As she retraced her steps, Bethan passed a man on a ladder, fixing a home-made banner over the porch of his house. The banner read *Southbeck Says No*.

There had been similar placards and posters in some of the cottage windows and gardens, all bearing slogans like *Save Our Village*, and more dramatically *We Will Fight For Our Children*.

Dismissing this as evidence of some local squabble, Bethan returned to Maggie's cottage. The air had cleared her head. She was here in Southbeck, she had a duty to Harvey, and she would go and look for Dyke Farm, which was marked on the map he had supplied.

She started the car, waved to the man at the end cottage who was watering his cabbages, then turned west into the open country. Every lane end had its message of defiance. *Hands Off Southbeck*, and *Don't Poison Our Earth*. One market-garden was fronted by a row of oil drums. Each bore a crudely-daubed word in white. *No Dumping Here*.

Smiling at this evidence of a strong community spirit, Bethan noted a wooden signpost with the words Dyke Farm. She glanced around at the rolling wolds, the scattered houses, the wide sky unsullied by smoke or pollution. This was a far cry from London, its clubs and crowded streets.

She ran the car down a one-track lane, and drew up at a yard where a man was herding cows into a shed. As she got out, a dog came bounding over to meet her. It was barking so ferociously that Bethan halted.

The man gave her a brief glance, but no more. Between them, the dog and the cows made too much noise for a voice to be heard. Bethan got back in the car, and sat waiting.

Minutes later, the cowman loomed up by the open window.

'Who you looking for?'

'I want to speak to Trash Morgan.'

'You mean Jake. He's not here.'

'When will he be back?'

'Dunno. He's mending a bridge. You a friend of his?'

'You could say that,' replied Bethan coolly.

'I suppose I could let you into the house,' said the cowman doubtfully.

Wait around for Trash Morgan when he might be ages?

'Where is this bridge?' she asked.

'Bottom end of Mile Acre, next to the old Linwell airfield.'

She must have looked perplexed.

'You can't take that car,' he said, pleased to have scored a point. 'Jake's got a truck with four-wheel drive. You'll have to walk.'

'Right,' said Bethan briskly, beginning to find a bit more resolution than hitherto. 'Show

15

me where.'

It was a fine evening; for that she was grateful, because the walk led her through rutted lanes and over farmland. But once she had spotted the airfield, it was not so hard. Grey hangars were flanked by row upon row of derelict wartime airforce buildings. There was a sad look about them, the feeling of an era gone for ever.

But the field was evidently still used for flying. Small planes stood on the tarmac, and at the end of the runway, wind socks lifted in the gentle breeze.

From the slight rise where she stood, Bethan spotted the stream, and the bridge where Morgan was working. He looked entirely different. A disreputable hat was jammed down on his head, his shirt-sleeves were rolled up, revealing strong, brown arms, and muddy waders encased his feet.

He was absorbed in his job, and for a split second she was tempted to turn and walk away. But curiosity won. She waited, the light behind her, not speaking.

After a minute dragged by, irritation began to niggle her. Surely the man had seen her. How could he avoid doing so when they were the only two people within a mile?

'Hi Jake,' she called out, sarcasm in her voice.

He looked up, but kept silent. Don't try that

16

game with me, Bethan told herself. She dropped down the grassy bank and moved to the edge of the stream.

'What are you doing?' she asked, trying to conceal her impatience at his rudeness.

'I should have thought it was obvious. The point is, what are *you* doing? Harvey sent you, I suppose.'

'Harvey's in hospital,' said Bethan crisply. 'He had a car accident. This was right after you so rudely didn't turn up for your appointment.'

He could take that any way he liked.

'Is he badly hurt?' There was genuine concern in his voice.

'He'll live—Jake.'

'The name bothers you, doesn't it?'

He stared at her hard.

'But why?' she asked.

'Because I'm really Jacob Morgan. But it's no handle for a pop-singer—and people down here take me for what I am.'

'So this is the real you, is it, splashing about in streams and humping lumps of wood?'

'Yes, probably. I needed time to think. Harvey should know that.'

And I should know that you're wasting my time, thought Bethan resignedly. For the man was as difficult and self-centred as ever. He had not really opened her eyes, merely confirmed her previous conclusions.

As she turned to leave, he called out to her

that she could ride back with him if she hung around for a while. She sat down on a patch of dry grass, watching the comings and goings at the airfield. The place fascinated her with its atmosphere of bygone days, stirring up memories of old stories told in her childhood; wartime heroes, and desperate fights for freedom.

When Morgan was finished, he stowed away his gear in a truck that stood some distance away. As they juddered back along a green lane, he talked to her calmly about caring for the countryside, about footpaths that had been there for centuries, about planning for the future. If he thought at all about Harvey Lime and the American contract, he gave no clue. When Bethan left him, he let her go a few strides, then called out 'Don't come back.'

She was furious. A mixture of anger and frustration filled her as she returned to the cottage. It was all very well for Harvey to tell her to nail Morgan, but some things were impossible. The man's character was contradictory. He wanted to have his cake and eat it.

Maybe he was his own worst enemy. He could be brutal—think of Alys—or he could care for issues like preserving the countryside. He had spiked her guns, because even if she produced the contract, he probably wouldn't sign it.

Sleep on it, Bethan told herself. Her own views on Morgan were too raw and tangled for logical thought. She was making coffee when she heard the noise of a loudspeaker van approaching along the lane. It stopped by the cottages. Words boomed out, destroying the quiet peace of the evening.

'Southbeck needs *you*. Don't let the village down. It's your future, your life. Guard it.'

Whatever it was, Bethan was sure it didn't concern her. A glance out of the window showed her a tall, good-looking man in his early thirties, talking to the old fellow who grew cabbages. A few minutes later there was a knock on her door.

Opening it, she found herself looking up into a strong handsome face, tanned by wind and weather. It was the man from the loudspeaker van, carelessly elegant in his smart though casual country clothes. His brown eyes met hers steadily, then melted to a smile.

'Hi there.' His voice was firm and sure. 'I'm Ray Allington, chairman of the village committee. Are you coming to the meeting tonight?'

'I shouldn't think so,' murmured Bethan, amused by this turn of events. 'I'm what you might call a bird of passage.'

'If you visit here, then you must have some interest. And we need all the support we can get.'

19

'Not from me,' said Bethan lightly. She could of course have closed the door, but something about the man held her, in a way that had taken her completely off her guard. She didn't wish to be drawn in, yet she didn't want him to go.

'You'll have seen the posters,' he went on, ignoring her comment. 'We won't tolerate radioactive waste being buried here, and we'll do all we can to stop it. This is good, rich land, and we plan to keep it that way. We owe it to our children, and our children's children.'

'I haven't any children, so it doesn't concern me.'

'It concerns everybody—I'm sorry, I don't know your name.'

'Bethan Blake.'

'Nine o'clock at the village hall.'

'You should try Jake Morgan,' said Bethan crisply.

'Jake's already on the committee. Bethan, please come.'

His smile would have melted a glacier. She found herself smiling back, drawn into the warmth of his enthusiasm. It was infectious, a world away from the superficial values and standards of her normal day-to-day.

'Maybe,' she said, wondering about a man who was so clearly honest, and yet so silver-tongued. For why should she be bothered with some timpot village meeting? Except that Ray Allington had intrigued her. It was a long

20

time since she had felt so drawn towards a man. Put him out of your mind, Bethan told herself. He's probably married, with children, or why should he be so concerned about their future?

But he made her restless. At half past eight, she changed into a dress and jacket, and freshened her make-up. Five minutes before nine, she cautiously entered the village hall. It was surprisingly full. All the seats at the back were taken, leaving spaces only at the front. Feeling slightly conspicuous, Bethan walked forward.

There were four people on the platform, bending over papers spread out on a table, Ray Allington, Jake Morgan, a bluff, red-faced man, and a plump woman who looked like a nurse.

Already wishing she hadn't come, Bethan felt Ray Allington's eyes rest on her for a moment. He left the platform, spoke with a man standing near the front, then they both came over to her.

'Glad you came,' said Ray. 'This is Captain Harris from the Air Base. He'll look after you.'

The Captain was in his fifties, a taut, upright man with the sort of eyes she associated with flyers. As Ray Allington went back to the platform, Bethan followed Captain Harris to seats in the second row. His manners were impeccable.

'Tell me what's happening,' she requested.

'Just confirming plans of action. People are unanimous—no dumping—and dump-day is

21

only a month away.'

'What does Ray Allington do?'

'You mean besides this? He owns a sugar-beet plant, and several flower-farms. His family have been here for generations!'

'He's a family man?'

'Certainly. Two boys, away at school. No mother, you see.'

Before anything else could be said, the meeting started, with reports of action taken to date and plans for further action. Pressure on government had led to clashes, and there had been a firm refusal either to postpone or drop plans for dumping.

To Bethan, an outsider, the village seemed a hotbed of activity. The whole issue was a rocket about to be fired.

'Interested in flying?' asked Captain Harris, as the meeting broke up.

'Why?' asked Bethan, intrigued.

'I go up most days. You're welcome to a spin. Things always look so much better from up there.'

'Thank you,' she said, delighted. There was no need to tell him that she wouldn't be here long enough.

'Coming back for a coffee?'

'Where?'

'To the Air Club. A few of us meet there.'

'I'd love to, but I've left my car at the cottage.'

'No problem. Go with me, and Ray will bring you back.'

People were drifting away, some of them exchanging greetings with Bethan and Captain Harris. Jake Morgan came down from the platform. Yards away from Bethan, he stopped and stared at her hard.

'A persistent little nuisance, aren't you? What makes you think that following me around is going to make any difference?'

A tide of anger rose in Bethan, staining her skin. Hot words rose to her lips. The arrogance of him, the sheer, bone-headed arrogance. Did he think that everything and everybody pivoted on him?

She bit her lip, conscious of Captain Harris. Morgan strode off, followed by a twittering crowd, obviously his admirers.

'What on earth's got into Jake?' muttered the Captain. 'He's usually so good-natured—the salt of the earth.'

Is he, thought Bethan? She kept silent as she walked outside and across the car-park to the Captain's Reliant Scimitar.

CHAPTER THREE

As they drove towards Linwell Air Club, the Captain took the bends with such speed that

23

Bethan caught her breath. He explained that the derelict area had been an RAF base during World War Two.

Rows of drab, one-storey buildings stood silently in the gathering dusk. All the windows were broken, crazy stove-pipes rusted, whilst weeds and nettles thrust their way through crumbling concrete. Vandals had daubed slogans on the damp, grey-green walls.

Bethan shivered.

'It's like a ghost town,' she whispered.

The Captain glanced at her curiously.

'Why d'you say that?'

'Somehow I can imagine how it used to be—full of life and urgency.'

He didn't answer, for they had come to a sign saying Linwell Air Club, Private, and minutes later he was parking the car. Bethan looked around with interest. In contrast to what they had seen, the clubhouse was smart and busy, flanked by an assortment of low buildings, with hangars further away. Small private planes stood on the tarmac.

Excitement flared in Bethan, something she had not felt for a long time.

'What sort of planes do you fly?' she asked.

'Any sort. Small ones mostly.'

'Are you a flying instructor?'

The Captain's eyes twinkled.

'Yes, among other things.'

They went inside to a spacious room, with a

bar at one end.

A few people Bethan recognised from the village hall were already there. She ran her eyes over them, looking for Ray Allington, but he hadn't yet come. Captain Harris found Bethan a seat by the window, and brought two cups of coffee.

'I never touch the hard stuff,' he said cheerily, with a nod at the bar. 'Got to keep a cool head on my shoulders.'

His manner of being so sure and jaunty about everything warmed Bethan to laughter. She smiled at him, realising she was enjoying herself in this new crowd and surroundings.

The Captain was yarning away about some of his experiences in instructing new pupils to fly, when Bethan, glancing through the window, saw a smart car arrive, then Ray Allington got out. As he entered, various people button-holed him with queries, but soon he came over to Bethan's table.

'Hi there—again,' he said, and although it was only three words, it was like a private joke.

'Hi,' replied Bethan, wondering how her voice could wobble over such a simple syllable. For there was a current of magnetism that drew them together. His eyes were steadily on her face, and she felt the rosy tingling under her skin.

'Are we making you welcome in Southbeck?'

It was a good voice, warm as sun on smiling

fields.

'Yes,' said Bethan. 'What a pity I'm not staying.'

'How long will you be here?'

'Until the weekend,' she replied, not having thought about it until now. 'I have to be back in London on Monday.'

'Back to a husband, or some lucky fellow?'

'No such person,' smiled Bethan.

'Come and meet some others.'

Ray slipped his hand under her elbow, and the warmth of it ran through her. She didn't mind much about meeting the others, so long as she could keep Ray Allington there beside her. What am I thinking of, she wondered? I only met him a few hours ago.

The group around the bar were a good-natured lot, some flying-club regulars, some invited guests, but all animated by the local controversy, and the plan to bury radioactive waste in the area. Although Ray spoke calmly, Bethan could sense the iron-hard determination in him.

A telephone rang, and the barman called Ray over. Captain Harris had gone, saying he had to be up at four-thirty a.m. Then Trash Morgan came in with a girl of about eighteen. When his eyes fell on Bethan, his face darkened with anger. She shared his dismay. She had even less wish to see him than he had to see her. He came straight to her.

26

'Your hide must be thicker than an elephant's,' he said curtly. 'Didn't I tell you I wanted time alone?'

She didn't know whether to answer him or not, and people in the bar were listening.

'I'll go,' she said, then realised she couldn't until Ray Allington was ready.

'How's Alys?' Trash Morgan lobbed the question at her like a hand-grenade.

'Alys?' echoed Bethan, harder than permafrost at the mention of that name. 'What do you care about Alys? You want time alone. You just said so.'

She could have picked up a bottle from the bar, and crashed it down on his wild red hair. His eyes defied her, hating her, resenting her, and yet with something in them that was none of these things.

Ray Allington was back, his expression mildly questioning.

'You two seem to be old aquaintances,' he said diplomatically.

'It's time for me to leave,' said Bethan, striving for the lightness of tone that Morgan had killed.

Ray steered her towards the door. She would tell him about Morgan, but not here, where ears were flapping. Outside, the air was cool on her burning face. I'm a fool, she told herself, to let that man upset me this way. Harvey was right. Personal feelings and business shouldn't mix.

Ray held the car door open, and stood over her a minute longer than was necessary. Then he got in beside her. He didn't start the engine straight away.

'I take it that you and Jake Morgan have already met?' His voice was gentle, and it was hardly a question.

Bethan smiled ruefully.

'Trash Morgan is the reason I'm in Southbeck. I'm personal assistant to his agent, Harvey Lime. Unfortunately, Harvey's in hospital, and a signature is needed on a contract. Morgan won't play ball.'

Allington was silent for a moment. At length he said, 'I can't imagine why he should be so rude. Nobody in Southbeck is going to be impressed.'

Bethan searched for words.

'He had an affair with my younger sister, Alys, when she was barely out of school. She—well, he treated her badly. Now every time he looks at me, he sees Alys.'

'So he acts like a boor. It's a side of him I hadn't seen before.'

'Artistic temperament,' countered Bethan. She didn't want to waste time talking about Morgan.

Ray drove in silence back to the village. Outside Maggie's cottage he stopped, and looked intently at Bethan.

'You've only been here a while, and already

you've got me worrying about you.'

She was tired, but his words were like warm drops of healing oil. It was a long time since anyone had said they were worried about her.

'I'm still glad I came,' she said.

'And so am I. I'll see you again.'

'Yes.' From the first moment she had seen him, Bethan had felt that here was a man with whom she could be totally honest. She knew she could trust him, and he would not let her down.

She waved from the window as he drove away, knowing that probably other curtains were twitching. She went straight to her bedroom, not expecting to sleep well, but fell asleep almost at once.

In the morning, she was sitting over breakfast when there was a knock on the door. She opened it to find a man in a green overall clutching a large arrangement of beautiful fresh flowers. He grinned at her from above the foliage.

'The boss says have a good day.'

'They're lovely,' replied Bethan, her voice light, although her eyes had misted. There was no need to ask who they were from.

She dawdled over arranging the blooms, putting off the time when she would telephone Harvey, for the cottage had a phone, and she had no excuse. Sound sense told her to squash down personal feelings, go and tackle Morgan,

29

ignore his protests, insist on his signature, and go back to London. But that was the trouble. She didn't want to go back.

When she put the call through to St. Stephen's Infirmary, she obtained Harvey's room almost immediately. Hearing her voice, he started a long account of the medical tests and investigations that were planned for him, as well as his treatment. He sounded morose and preoccupied.

'Perhaps I shouldn't bother you,' murmured Bethan apologetically. 'But I'm not making much headway here.'

'With Morgan?' Harvey groaned. 'The last thing I need just now is ungrateful clients. Tell him I'll kick him from here to kingdom come if he doesn't say yes.'

That made her smile, although her doubts were still there.

'You can do it,' coaxed Harvey, sensing her hesitation. 'Try guile. If that doesn't work, well—'

He was right, and she owed it to Harvey to back him up as much as she could, and let him convalesce in peace. Before her resolve should weaken, Bethan put the black leather document-case in her car, and drove to Dyke Farm. This time there was no one in the yard, and the house door stood open.

Bethan walked in. In answer to her 'Anyone there?' an elderly woman poked her head

30

around the kitchen door. She seemed flustered, and faintly affronted by an unexpected presence.

'I must see Jake Morgan,' said Bethan firmly. 'He knows me, and he knows what this is about.'

'Oh yes?' The woman's mouth became a thin line. She was obviously a faithful member of the Trash Morgan fan club. 'Well Mr. Morgan's not here. He's gone on one of his walkabouts, and nobody knows when he'll be back.'

'Oh no,' Bethan exclaimed in annoyance. Part of Trash Morgan's image was that from time to time he slung a few things in a rucksack, struck off into the countryside, and slept under trees and stars.

Well, that was it. Morgan had led them by the nose over this deal, and Harvey or no Harvey, Bethan didn't mean to waste another minute on it. She left Dyke Farm, and drove around for a while to simmer down. When she got back to Maggie's cottage, an envelope had been slipped through the letter-box. Inside was a white card, headed with the address Wood Hall, Southbeck. On it, in a firm hand, were written the words 'Come to dinner tonight, about seven, Ray.'

For once, Bethan agonised over what to wear, how much make-up to use, for this wasn't London, and a show-biz crowd. She wanted to look good for Ray Allington, yet she had only

31

brought a few clothes with her. The last thing she had expected in Southbeck was a date with a man who had walked into her life like the sun coming up.

She settled for a white dress, with black belt, and long black beads, knowing she looked gamin and too thin: elegant, a woman with some experience, but not too much.

Unsure of where Wood Hall was located, Bethan turned for help to the other person she knew in Southbeck—Captain Harris. The directory gave the number of Linwell Flying Club, and she heard the barman calling for the Captain to come to the phone. She was in luck. Moments later his brisk voice said 'Hello'.

'It's Bethan Blake, and I need to know how to get to Wood Hall,' she explained.

It occurred to her that she could have telephoned Ray himself, but now it was too late.

'Ray's asked you to Wood Hall?' He sounded surprised.

She murmured an affirmation.

'Go into the village, past the church, then head for Cherry Heath. About a mile along you'll come to a copse of beeches. You're there.'

She thanked him, and he replied by repeating his offer of taking her up for a spin, when she felt like it.

'I might just do that.' Bethan smiled as she

replaced the receiver.

Driving towards Cherry Heath her heart was singing. The copse of beeches stood out against the skyline as she approached. A driveway ran round in front of a mellow stone house, with thick walls and tall chimneys. Wide windows looked onto green lawns, with banks of yellow roses. Clematis entwined the pillars of the front porch.

It was an impressive place, standing on its own, surrounded by rich land. Bethan's heart missed a beat as Ray opened the door and came out to greet her. His clothes, like his surroundings, were impeccable, and he wore them with careless ease.

'Thank you for the lovely flowers,' she said.

'My pleasure. You've brightened up the dullness.'

Bethan laughed.

'Things don't seem any too dull around here, with protests, and marches, and all the rest.'

'Come inside,' he urged her. They went into a wood-panelled hall, where solid furniture gleamed with loving care. He led her to a comfortable sitting-room, where French windows opened out onto the lawn. Through an archway was a dining-room.

'Who looks after all this?' asked Bethan, gazing around in admiration.

'My daily housekeeper, Mrs. Challis. She's been like a second mother to the boys since—'

He broke off, and handed her a drink in a delicate glass. His lean face had a clouded look.

'Your boys,' Bethan gently prompted.

'Away at school. Richard is ten, and Tom is eight.'

A shadow had fallen, and Bethan knew that Ray was striving to dispel it. He took her through to the dining-room, where a delicious cold meal was waiting.

'If this is what Mrs. Challis can do, she's a treasure,' said Bethan admiringly.

Bit by bit the atmosphere lightened again, until they were chatting and joking as though they had known each other all their lives. And that was how it felt.

She helped him stack the dish-washer in an airy kitchen, and wondered what he had in mind for the rest of the evening. Bethan sensed that Ray was aching to talk, yet it was too soon in their relationship, and maybe he wasn't the sort of man to reveal his thoughts anyway.

'Have you a photograph of your sons?' she asked.

'Yes. In my study.'

He crossed the hall, opened a door, and went in. Minutes passed. Bethan drifted after him.

He was sorting through a drawer, in a room with a desk, shelves of books, maps and graphs on the walls, a collection of Second World War memorabilia at one end. The photographs were all of Air Force Flyers, and their warplanes.

Neat labels showed names, dates, decorations for valour.

Their young, eager faces drew Bethan towards them. Down the years they stared at her, their eyes looking towards some distant victory, frozen in a moment of time.

Her eyes moved from one picture to another, steadily reading dates and figures. She came back to one picture, a pilot in his thirties, with a calm and steady face.

Her heart somersaulted as she swayed on her feet.

Ray was beside her.

'What's wrong?'

'Nothing. Someone walked over my grave.'

CHAPTER FOUR

'You look pale.' His voice was concerned. 'It's warm in here. Let me open a window.'

Bethan stood subdued, a little detached from what was going on, because she didn't understand it. The faded photographs of airmen that lined the walls of Ray Allington's study showed men who had been pilots, navigators, bomb-aimers in World War Two, all of them strangers. Except one: a man in his late thirties, with receding dark hair, and flaring eyebrows. A face she had known since her childhood.

Ray grasped her shoulders, and looked anxiously into her eyes.

'Now tell me what it is,' he said.

'You've made a study of wartime flyers?' she ventured.

'Yes, I have. My father was a pilot, and I grew up listening to his stories. He was one of the lucky ones. He came back.'

Bethan smiled faintly.

'My father wasn't a flyer, but his older brother was. And this brother didn't come back; in fact, he went missing and there was never any official explanation of his fate. He's there on the wall looking at me. His name was David Blake.'

In one sharp moment it had all come back. Bethan's father, Vernon, had possessed a deep and undying affection for his older brother, some of it hero-worship, some family pride, and David's disappearance had caused an aching emptiness that touched not only Vernon, but the next generation also.

'Blake. But of course.' Ray gazed at her in realisation. 'Who would have thought you had the same family tree.'

It was sad, but it was a long time ago, and there was nothing anyone could do about it now. Vernon Blake was dead, and the only two remaining members of the Blake family were Bethan and Alys.

'I'll make you a hot drink,' Ray offered, and

whilst he did so, Bethan looked at photographs of his sons, the older one dark-eyed and serious, the younger one fair-haired and chubby.

The evening had melted away. She didn't want to leave, and she knew Ray felt the same. But enough had happened, and tonight, odd as it had been, had spelled out to Bethan that both of them had others for whom they had responsibility.

She stood up to go. He walked outside with her, and in the warm darkness, in a moment of shared understanding, she buried her head against his shoulder, drawing comfort from his strength and sincerity.

'We have something going for us, you know that,' he said, his hand gently brushing her hair.

'Yes. I know.'

She drove home in a dream, thankful for a quiet country road. She lay in bed, eyes wide, staring at the ceiling, conscious of a miracle, a change, a milestone in her life. She fell asleep, slept late, and woke to hear someone banging on the cottage door. It was Ray, picnic hamper in the car, impatient to take her to the coast, so that they could smell the sea, and feel the salt breezes. They had a perfect day. On Sunday evening she drove back to London.

Her own flat, pleasant though it was, seemed strangely empty. Voices echoed in her head, faces swam up in front of her eyes. The fresh sea breezes had made her healthily tired, yet every nerve in her body felt vibrant, twanging with life.

Although it was late, Bethan searched out the box of faded family photographs and papers, all that was left of former years. Pictures of her mother and father stirred old memories; Alys and Bethan as carefree children; David Blake in his air-force uniform; and a yellowed newspaper cutting that detailed the non-return of a bomber plane and crew, which had disappeared, never been reported shot down, or crashed.

In the last few days, Bethan had moved a long way out of her normal channel. Tomorrow she must contact Harvey, tell him bluntly about Morgan and his vanishing tricks, get back to shouldering her work.

Next day she was in the office early, checking on what was urgent and making a barrage of telephone calls. Then she went to St. Stephen's Infirmary.

Harvey was sitting hunched up in a chair, wearing a plum-coloured dressing-gown that only emphasised the pallor of his skin. Bethan felt a stab of concern, which was disguised under a smile. He brightened up, and demanded a full report, some colour returning to his face as he became more animated.

When Bethan raised the subject of Morgan, Harvey was almost apathetic. Maybe his accident had quenched him, maybe hospital routine had dulled the urgency of his daily life. All he said was, 'The man's a fool. There's no money in fresh air.'

It wasn't like Harvey to let a contract slip through his fingers, and it told Bethan that he had bigger worries. Harvey wasn't one to reveal much about his private life, but his wife Mary had no such restraint. Bethan resolved to telephone her later, meanwhile entertaining Harvey with a spiced-up version of her venture into village politics, and the goings-on in Southbeck.

He was highly amused, joking with her about the straw in her hair and the cow-dung on her boots.

'Does your sister use the cottage often?' asked Bethan.

'Maggie? She's gone to Australia to stay with her son for three months. I'm keeping an eye on the place while she's away but you can do that for me. Go there when you wish, just so long as you let me know.'

It had fallen into Bethan's lap as though fate had meant it. She thanked him, and offered payment, but the offer was brushed aside. She left the hospital in a thoughtful mood, realising that Harvey would not be back at work for a while.

A phone call to Mary confirmed this. Although his injuries from the accident were not serious, examination had revealed that he

39

had a chronic heart condition. A programme of treatment was being sorted out, and Harvey was having to adjust his ideas to this.

The week went by, curiously flat for Bethan, although there were the usual alarms and moments of crisis. On Friday, she closed the office in the early afternoon and drove to Southbeck. The woman who occupied the middle cottage came out with a duster, and shouted 'Hello'. When Bethan called a greeting back, the woman asked if she needed any fresh milk. Bethan said it might be handy, and the woman offered to leave a bottle on the doorstep.

Already the place was drawing her to it. The small encounter, trivial though it was, pleased and amused her. She hadn't much idea how she was going to spend the next two days, but Bethan had a strong feeling that they would take shape on their own. One thing she had decided—to contact Captain Harris and accept his offer of a flight. In some way she didn't quite understand, seeing the picture of war pilot David Blake had triggered this.

About nine o'clock she telephoned Linwell Air Club. Captain Harris was delighted to hear her voice. When she made a tentative enquiry, he offered immediately.

'Tomorrow morning, but it will have to be early.'

'How early?'

'Seven o'clock.'

40

'I'll be there,' she promised.

She went to bed, and dreamed of running across tarmac to clamber into a small plane that was waiting. It took off the moment she was on board, but when she looked at the pilot's seat, it was empty. She was alone, heading into the night sky, with no one to turn to, no one to save her.

When she woke, skeins of nightmare still threaded her mind, but it was a beautiful morning, calm and radiant, with a cloudless sky. Bethan put away foolish fancies, dressed in a smart track-suit, ate a light breakfast, and headed for Linwell Air Club.

Although the day was so young, already cars were parked by the clubhouse. With an assurance she was not sure she felt, Bethan walked into the reception area. Various doors led off this section, most of them open, and in one of these rooms, a sheaf of papers in his hand, Captain Harris stood talking to another man.

Seeing her, he waved, and beckoned her in. With a screeching noise, he dragged up a chair for her. The other man left.

'Morning, m'dear. Right on time, so full marks for that. Now you're quite sure you want to do this? You might not like flying in a small, two-seater plane.'

He was brisk and friendly, but different from the last time when they had met. Suddenly she

41

knew that he was a man who flew because it was the only thing that made sense to living. His previous remark came back to her. Things always look so much better from up there.

'I'm quite sure,' she said firmly. If this was a new, wider world, she wanted to know what it was all about, what it was like to feel the freedom of the skies. David Blake had known it. She could not hope to even touch on his experience. But she could try for something, however little.

After he had made notes in a book, Captain Harris took her outside to where a two-seater monoplane was waiting on the concrete. It looked small and flimsy. Excitement fluttered in Bethan's chest like a bird.

He walked around the plane making checks, then when they had climbed inside and fastened their belts he asked her, 'Do you just want a spin, or shall I tell you what goes on?'

'Tell me,' she requested.

With a smile of amusement he explained the control panel, then the propeller began spinning as the engine growled into life. They taxied down a concrete apron and swung onto the runway. The noise built up and up. Then—the moment. Cramped shoulder to shoulder with Captain Harris, blackness rushed up to meet Bethan, and white light blinded her.

They were airborne—they had slipped their chains, and the whole, beautiful world was their kingdom.

The landscape swung below as the aircraft climbed away from the earth. Through the cloud-shot wonder in her mind, Bethan was conscious of the Captain's calm voice. She looked down on cornfields, farm buildings like dolls' houses, a river winding like a silver-grey ribbon. Her pulse steadied, and her heart stopped racing.

But the exhilaration, the sheer, raw excitement, was there. Time ceased to exist. When she realised he was heading back to base, it was with a douche of disappointment.

'Like it?' Captain Harris asked with a smile, as they climbed out onto solid ground.

'I think I could grow to like it very much.'

'We'll see you then?'

He had already given her an hour of his time. Bethan thanked him, as he headed for the building he said, 'A pity Ray's not around today. He'll be sorry he missed you.'

All Bethan's newly-found pleasure evaporated.

'Is he away?' she asked, feigning casualness.

'It's sports day at his sons' school.'

Now the hours stretched ahead of her, empty as a desert. Maybe it was foolish of her to have been so optimistic about seeing Ray. He had, as she had discovered, many responsibilities and commitments. She felt forlorn as a lost child.

In the cottage, she sat gloomily over a meal

and a cup of coffee, reproaching herself for being naïve. Ray had been kind to her, pleasant and attentive. He had sent her flowers, and given her a glorious day's romp in the sunshine. But he had made no further date or contact. In spite of the closeness she had instinctively felt between them, doubts now assailed her.

He had sons, but where was his wife? How could Bethan and Ray have anything going for them, unless she knew more about their true situation?

There was the rest of the day to fill. She carried out a deckchair, and set it in a pleasant corner of the walled garden. With the sun warm upon her face, everything was peaceful. Presently, her eyelids drooped.

The heavy click of a car door came to Bethan as from a long way off. For a second her heart soared wildly, hoping against hope. Then common sense told her that Ray couldn't possibly be here at this time, for it was early afternoon, and school sports would still be in full swing.

She closed her eyes again, but something stopped her sinking back into the aimless apathy of before. The mood—imperfect though it had been—had gone. The atmosphere prickled. The sense of aloneness had vanished.

Bethan's eyes jerked open, and she found herself looking straight into the unsmiling face of Trash Morgan. He stood motionless, a few yards away, staring at her. His brooding eyes burned in his thin face. A shiver ran over Bethan's skin. He looks haunted, she thought. Like Heathcliff.

All her old dislike began to smoulder. She had taken one disappointment today over Ray, and the last thing she wanted now was a clash with Morgan. Everything about him spelled trouble. It always had.

She sighed audibly, blaming him for shattering what peace she had.

'I want to talk to you,' he said.

'About the contract?' She managed to sound supercilious.

'No. About Alys.'

Bethan stood up.

'Go away,' she said angrily. 'Go—away!'

'I will not go away,' he said, deliberately emphasising his words. 'Not until I've found out what I want to know.'

Bethan was trembling. In the honeysuckle hedge, a bee buzzed drowsily from flower to flower.

CHAPTER FIVE

She faced him, trying to control her anger. This day, on which she had started out in such hope, had become a shambles.

45

'You have a nerve,' she said scathingly. 'You knew Harvey sent me chasing after you those other times, but not now. I'm *not* here on business, I'm here for my own reasons. So the sooner you leave, the better.'

'Not before you've told me about Alys.'

'Goodbye, Morgan.'

'It's no use. You won't get rid of me like that.'

He perched himself on a small stone wall. Although his skin was tanned with sun and wind, his eyes were sunken, as though he was short of sleep. His shoulders hunched forward, determination in every line of him.

A throbbing silence ensued, broken only by the bright chirping and rustling of birds, and the sound of a lawn-mower in someone else's garden.

Bethan sighed in exasperation, tempted to stalk into the house and slam the door. But even if she did, Morgan would still be there.

'This is ridiculous,' she snapped. 'You act like a child throwing tantrums; then you turn up here as though nothing had happened.'

'Where is Alys?'

'Alys has a new life now.'

'I'll find her, y'know. But it would be easier if you'd help.'

'You—will—what?'

'I'll find her.'

Disquiet, like some creeping infection, ran

46

over Bethan's skin. His voice had the ring of utter conviction. She drew in a thin breath, and tried to steady her voice.

'Alys is miles away. Why should you want to see her now? Leave her alone. Just leave her alone.'

'I want to help her. I miss her. In fact, I miss her like hell. Can't you see? I'm lonely.'

'Lonely?' Bethan gazed at him in amazement. 'You with your razzamatazz, and hordes of women after you?'

'There's no lasting joy in that kind of life, although people don't believe it.'

'Grow up, Morgan,' said Bethan curtly.

'I am doing. And it's painful.'

It dawned on her that she was doing what she had said she would not do—talking to Morgan, and discussing this matter. He's canny, she told herself. Astute. Tricky. But there was an uneasy feeling that this time he wasn't playing a part, he was peeling off a layer, and revealing the real man.

'Tell me about the baby,' he said abruptly.

'There's nothing to tell.'

'Was it a boy or a girl?'

'A boy.'

He was silent again, a palpable aura of solitariness about him. Harden your heart, Bethan told herself. Too much had happened.

'All I want is Alys's address,' he said quietly.

He sounded concerned, reasonable. Suddenly

47

Bethan had a picture of Alys weeping bitterly, choking out the words 'He doesn't love me. He doesn't love me.'

'I'll think about it,' she replied, knowing that even conceding such a possibility, she had weakened. 'Now you'll have to excuse me. I'm going indoors. The sun's given me a headache.'

It was only partly the sun, but he left, with no more argument. Bethan went upstairs and lay on the bed, grateful for the cool pillow against her burning face. She dozed lightly, her mind escaping to the vast expanse of clear, cloudless sky, the place where problems vanished, and the earth was left behind.

She must have slept for several hours, for when she awoke it was evening and the telephone was ringing. Still bleary from sleep, she picked up the receiver and the welcome voice of Ray Allington bathed her in a warm ocean of words. He sounded so gently teasing, so assured that tears stung her eyes.

Do I need him so much, she asked herself silently? Maybe she did. Maybe the bright, empty life that had seemed to fill her needs had done nothing of the sort.

'How did you know I was here?' she ventured.

'I took a detour past the cottage and saw your car. There's still time for a snack and a drink, if you've no other plans.'

She wanted to tell him that he had made her

48

day, but contented herself with 'See you,' and when he arrived half an hour later, the rest of the day seemed as nothing else but a tedious preparation for this glorious moment.

Surprising herself, she found she was talking about Morgan, telling Ray of his threat to track down Alys and the baby.

'I know it sounds childish,' she confessed, 'but I can't bear the thought of him stirring up any more trouble. Alys was so devastated—now she has a new beginning, and I don't want anything spoiling that.'

'Where is Alys?'

'In Vancouver. She got a job as a nursemaid with a fairly well-heeled family, who were glad of an English girl, and were prepared to accommodate her, along with little Dan.'

Ray reached for Bethan's hand.

'Don't let it get to you like that. After all, they're grown-up people. It's really up to them, not you.'

Bethan's fingers stiffened. Ray's was the voice of reason, but she was not sure she appreciated it.

'He was pretty mean to her. That's what I can't forget.'

'Then maybe he's sorry. I've usually found Jake a decent bloke, and he loves children. Some people are hopeless with them, but he's one of the other sort. They go to him like lambs. My own boys think he's great.'

49

There was no answer to that, and this conversation, instead of unburdening her, had provoked uncomfortable feelings. Her loyalty to Alys seemed suddenly to have isolated her. Striving to dispel the shadows, Bethan asked, 'Where are we going?'

'To a little waterside inn, where we can watch the ducks and boats come in.'

The place was delightful, and when they sat where willow trees bent to the water, Bethan's doubts drifted away, as she felt in Ray the things she had scarcely known she was seeking.

'When shall I meet your boys?' she asked.

'Do you want to meet them?'

His brown eyes searched her face. The answer was important.

'Yes,' she said. 'I don't know if I can live up to Morgan's reputation, but I shan't know, shall I, unless I try?'

If there was a shade of sarcasm in the words, Ray ignored it, and told her the date when the school term would be over; then said, 'Could a girl like you be happy away from city lights?'

These few words again held a wealth more meaning than it appeared, and Bethan was suddenly brimming with the sheer joy of living.

'I love it here,' she assured him. 'I've got a feeling that by some twist of fate I've landed exactly where I belong.'

He drove her home, stopping in a lane overhung with horse-chestnut blossom to take

50

her in his arms and kiss her over and over again. As his lips stirred up feelings that had been dormant, drawing them through her body until they reached an almost unbearable pitch of longing, Bethan found herself aching for the sweet, sensuous pleasure of full surrender. The flame between them was small now, but it could soon be a roaring furnace.

'You're beautiful,' he whispered, his hands moving in wonder over her body. 'If only you knew how long I've waited, and how hard it's been.'

Every drop of Bethan's blood yearned for the fulfilment of the loving act of a man and his chosen woman. But the car was cramped, and Ray was too sensitive to hurry things along too fast. They sat for a while, holding hands, content just to be together.

It was past midnight when he took her back to the cottage. Reluctantly he prepared to let her go.

'What about a bit of legwork in the morning?' he asked jokingly.

'Legwork?'

'Yes. Getting around, delivering handbills, stirring things up for our stand against the dumpers. People here care very strongly about their village.'

'I'm an outsider,' she said, more to test him than anything.

'But you don't mean to stay that way. I'll

collect you.'

She smiled, he won, and arranged to pick her up the following day.

Bethan slept peacefully, woke early, set the cottage to rights, and was ready, kitted out in anorak, jeans and trainers, when Ray appeared. He ran an appreciative eye over her. And I imagined I was sophisticated, she thought, as the hint of a blush warmed her face.

In spite of her doubts, she enjoyed the morning's activities, gaining quiet amusement from the kindly but curious reception given by the villagers they visited. Country folk they might be, but there wasn't much they missed.

One comfortably-spreading matron, sitting on a bench shelling peas, looked Bethan over, then remarked, 'Those be two fine boys that Mr. Allington 'as. Like children, do you?'

'Love them,' replied Bethan sturdily.

If someone had asked her that question a month ago, she would have thought they were mad. Now she was into something that she had never contemplated. Perhaps she was on trial in more senses than one. The idea stirred something in her that went to the very roots.

She wanted Ray, badly enough to learn to understand his way of life, his hopes, his plans. We've got something going for us, he had said. Bethan meant to hang on to that.

At lunch-time they returned to Wood Hall, planning to cut up hunks of bread and cheese, but Captain Harris and half a dozen Air Club friends turned up with an outdoor barbeque and all the food that went with it.

Bethan found herself grilling steaks alongside a six-foot tall Amazon of a girl, with a mane of shaggy blonde hair tied up in a swishing ponytail. Her name was Julie, and she looked magnificent, a raw, untamed creature, with fire in her blood.

How could any man fail to find her attractive, Bethan wondered? But Ray, although unfailingly courteous, seemed unaffected by Julie's charms.

The pleasant garden, the hum of conversation, the delicious odour of food, suddenly gave Bethan a buzz of pure happiness. She was glad to be here, glad to have slipped her city chains, glad to have stepped out of past heartache.

'Isn't it all gorgeous?' she said, turning to Julie with a huge smile.

'Super. I'm really hungry after this morning.'

'What was it this morning?'

'Two hours flying with Perc. I'm going solo soon.'

'You fly?' Bethan gazed at her in respectful awe.

'Sure. I'm getting my private pilot's licence.'

She sounded as though there was no doubt at all.

'Who's Perc?' asked Bethan.

'Captain Harris. He doesn't like it, so he doesn't generally tell.'

Food disappeared, wine was produced, then Bethan and Julie made coffee. The afternoon drifted by.

Something started for me here in this house, thought Bethan. It started when I stood face to face with David Blake.

When Captain Harris was leaving, Bethan waylaid him.

'I've had a wonderful idea,' she said. 'Will you teach me how to fly?'

'Are you serious?'

'Absolutely.'

'Come and see me, and we'll talk about it.'

Through the cheery goodbyes and departures, Bethan became chillingly conscious of the closed look on Ray's face. As though the sun had gone in.

She started carrying coffee-mugs back into the house, uneasy and puzzled by the drop in temperature. Ray went into his study and closed the door, not speaking. What's wrong, she thought, bewildered? What have I done?

The silence of Wood Hall yawned around her. This is silly, she told herself. But the shut door seemed a barrier, a rejection. She was aimlessly flipping through a magazine when he reappeared.

'You'll need to get back,' was all he said, heading for the car outside.

54

'Ray—what is it?'

Bethan followed him anxiously.

'Don't talk. Just get in.'

His face was grim and pale.

'If I've upset you—' she began, but the shutters had come down, and his silence was a stony wall.

The drive back to Maggie's cottage was uncomfortable, such a contrast to their earlier bright pleasure that Bethan wanted to crawl away and hide.

When he got out to open the door for her, she leaned across and said, 'If you'll just tell me.'

'I can't talk about it,' Ray replied curtly. 'Not now.'

He left, with no softening, no suggestion for their next meeting. Bethan went indoors, numb with disappointment. The shining bubble of her day had burst. Emotions battled in her, perplexity at this sharp turn of events, anger at Ray for hurting her. Whatever the reason, she was back on her own, rejected.

Hurt pride whispered, 'Get in your car and leave. Go back to London. Walk away.' But her empty flat seemed as attractive as a prison cell. To calm her furious thinking, and also partly to repay Harvey Lime, Bethan got out gardening tools, and flung herself into a session of weeding and trimming. But although it exhausted her physically, her mind was still racing.

She washed, crawled to bed, longing to shut

out her thoughts. She dozed, and woke after nine o'clock when the light was going. Bethan knew she would not sleep again for hours, so pulled on her anorak and trainers, determined to walk.

Outside, the air was cool and fresh, with dusk blurring the outlines in soft, approaching darkness. There was a balm in the twilight, as though it drew her and held her. Subconscious will took her through lanes and byways in the direction of the flying club.

Her intentions were unclear. Maybe she just meant to wander around, absorbing the atmosphere, familiarising herself with the place, although of course it was private property.

Lights glimmered from the clubhouse, and the runway lights made a pathway for returning travellers. It was all there—the magic, the fascination. No sound broke the stillness as Bethan padded silently past the derelict RAF huts of yesterday. Broken windows gaped. A door hung creaking.

Then, blurred in the half-light, she saw a man come hurrying towards her. She stopped as he approached, perturbed by the urgency of his movement. As he grew nearer, she saw that he wore bloodstained flying-gear, one sleeve torn, though his head was bare, and his face smudged with dirt. But it was the desperation in him, the sheer, naked misery that riveted her.

'I've got to get back to base,' he gasped.

'Which way? Which way is it?'

Bethan gasped and drew back at the sight of his sunken eyes, full of their own nightmares. Then the note of a light plane broke into the shuddering silence, the strong, steady engine noise of someone coming in to land.

She looked again, and the man was gone.

CHAPTER SIX

Bewildered, she strained her eyes into the gathering gloom. She had been distracted for only a moment, and in that time the man had vanished. Her head sang with the sound of the plane coming home.

As the darkness fell around her, Bethan stood, all movement frozen. Fear did not touch her, but time had locked her in a capsule where there was no past and no future, only a vast eternity, where everything merged, and blurred together.

Blinking her eyes, she saw people moving on the runway, car headlights beaming. She shivered, as cold rose up in her, convulsing her legs and arms, making her teeth chatter. It came into her head with stabbing clarity that it was foolish, maybe even dangerous, to be hanging around the old camp, here in the darkness on her own.

Back at the cottage, Bethan had no recollection of how she had arrived there. Her head felt light and empty, her body slow and clumsy, as though she had run many miles. Shivering still, she ran a bath, and soaked gratefully in the warm water.

Some composure returned, but as she dried herself, and crept into bed, it seemed that in some way she didn't understand, the fragile bubble of her hopes had burst.

She slept badly, haunted by the vision of a distraught airman, who had appealed to her for help, in vain. In the morning, she packed her few belongings, and drove back to London. Work tomorrow.

Once inside office walls, a seething mass of urgent business consumed her. Clients sat in the waiting-room, the telephone scarcely stopped ringing. Stall them, Harvey had said, but that had been a short-term solution, and nothing was going to stop whilst he lay in St. Stephen's Infirmary.

When at last there was a lull, Bethan telephoned Mary Lime, to get the latest report on the patient. It was far from cheering. Artery trouble, building up for years, had been diagnosed, and there was the prospect of an operation. With sinking heart, Bethan supplied a sympathetic ear as Mary told it in detail.

Harvey, most probably, wasn't going to be back for months. Mary, sensing Bethan's dismay, said, 'It's likely that Mark will step in, until we sort something out. But he has his own business, and naturally, he can't just—'

Listening with half her mind, Bethan saw that nothing was going to be quite the same from now. Mark Lime was a younger edition of his father, suaver, more into money than talent. Everything was changing. Everything.

She visited Harvey, assuring him that things were running smoothly at the office, listening to her own voice, which called up all the insincere promises and evasions of her job. Leaving him, she went back to the flat to change. Harvey had secured a succession of one-night bookings at hotels and exhibitions for two northern sisters who sang country and western songs. They were good, they were raw, and nervous of the London breakthrough, so Harvey wanted Bethan along as mother hen.

She sat by her mirror, lining her eyes with black, reflecting that the shadows made her face look haggard. The ghost-grey dress only emphasised her pallor. But nobody cared tuppence how she looked, she reflected bitterly.

Alys was six thousand miles away. She had no one else. Only in this last month had she begun to see how isolated she was.

Sturdy independence reared, as Bethan reminded herself of how much she had fought and clawed her way up on the promotion ladder to achieve her present success. Not long ago, it had seemed everything. Now it seemed less, much less than enough.

Bethan tracked the two sisters down, in a room at the back of a lavish hotel, where the car-park was already choked. The girls were eye-catchers in their high boots and white leather skirts, and jackets trimmed with gold chains.

Full marks for appearance, thought Bethan, who never missed a point when it came to assessing potential. A pity I'm not so good at it in other respects, she reflected ruefully.

Of the two singers, the older one was brash, almost to the point of setting Bethan's teeth on edge, but the younger one, who looked a shade anorexic, was almost rigid with nerves.

Bethan went into her act of cheerful confidence, forgetting everything else. When the time came for the musical spot, she began to wonder if perhaps there wasn't a bit of the old magic left after all: the lights, the crowd, the melodies. Except that looking at the young girl singer, who had a yearning intensity, put her so painfully in mind of Alys.

The week flew past, work being the anodyne, and leaving little time for personal regrets, except when she returned to her flat each night alone.

As the weekend drew near, she shelved any plans to go to the cottage, although in this decision there was conflict. Meeting Captain

Harris and the Air Club crowd had revealed a side of Bethan's nature that had been hidden: the pull of the skies, the excitement of flying.

All those stories told to her in her childhood by her father about pilot David Blake had been like seeds germinating in the dark.

At Linwell Air Club she had come face to face with reality. It seemed as though fate was handing her an opportunity too good to miss. She was a single woman with a well-paid job. If flying lessons added a little zest and colour to life, why shouldn't she try?

But the rift with Ray had hurt her. Bethan couldn't explain it, which made it worse. Previous to that, he hadn't said he loved her, but he had certainly hinted at a permanent relationship. What then had gone wrong?

This weekend she would spend Saturday in town, shopping for a new outfit, then killing the evening by using a complimentary stalls seat at a theatre showing a play that had been panned by the critics, but which the public had made into a rip-roaring success.

On Sunday, determined not to sit around and brood, she took a trip out to Hampstead Heath, but although it was a glorious day, with all the evidence of summer, her heart was somewhere else.

When she returned to her flat, the hall porter was looking out for her.

'You had a visitor,' he reported. 'Gentleman

61

up from the country. He said to tell you he waited as long as he could.'

Just my luck, thought Bethan in dismay. It only emphasised what a wash-out this couple of days on her own had been. London, with all its bright lights, had worn thin. For Bethan now, the real colour, the real action, was somewhere else.

She suddenly recalled Trash Morgan and his farm. With a kind of understanding, she saw that perhaps there could be crosscurrents in his life, powers that pulled him in different directions. He could command the glamour, and the notoriety, and yet he sought simpler values.

A letter had been pushed under her door. It said 'Bethan' on the envelope, and at once she recognised Ray Allington's writing, from the note he had sent her at the cottage. She made herself a cup of coffee, and sat down to read it.

Wood Hall,
Southbeck.
June 21st.

Dear Girl,

I have missed you this weekend, and am sorry if I am the reason. We still have lots to learn about each other, and need to sit down and talk.

If you can, will you have dinner with me next Friday evening? Then on Saturday I will bring the boys to Southbeck so that you can meet them.

Say yes.

R.

Bethan lay in bed, the note still in her hand. The words were direct, non-sentimental. But they told her all she needed to know. He wanted to see her, and he planned for her to meet his sons. In the morning, she addressed an envelope to him, took a sheet of paper, and wrote the single word 'Yes'.

Mellowed with happiness, she wrote a brief note to Morgan, passing on Alys's address. Ray perhaps was right. They were grown-up people. It was really up to them.

In the following days Mark Lime demanded a good deal of Bethan's time, but she told him that she intended to take Friday afternoon off.

She drove to the cottage with a heady sense of going home. Just before seven o'clock Ray telephoned, arranging to pick her up in half an hour. He sounded cheerful and loving. It seemed an age since she had seen him, and she couldn't wait to be with him.

When he arrived, his eyes lingered appreciatively on her pale, rose-pink dress, its neckline beaded with pearls.

'You look like a morning sunrise,' he said. 'Sparkling and new.'

Suddenly, that was exactly how she felt. As

though everything up to now had been just a rehearsal for the real show.

'Where are we going?' she asked.

'To The Angel, at Herncaster. An ideal place for lovers.'

If there had been a cloud between them, he didn't show it. For lovers, she thought, tasting the word. For us. Bethan and Ray.

Throughout the drive, on quiet country roads, he spoke little, but she was content to wait. The Angel had gleaming windows in white-painted frames looking out onto a cobbled courtyard with rustic tables and chairs. Tubs of flowers in a riot of summer colours lined the pathway.

Like a wedding, thought Bethan, then reproached herself for a thought that had been born naturally.

'It's lovely,' she said, as they were shown into a sumptuously-carpeted lounge, where bright copper and brass glowed on the highly-polished furniture.

Ray ordered drinks, and they studied the menu, although Bethan doubted if she could eat anything. All she wanted was to sit and look at Ray. His lean, brown face, with the crinkle of lines at the corner of his eyes, already seemed incredibly precious to her.

What's happening to me, she marvelled? In the course of a career that had witnessed all manner of other people's affairs, couplings, dirty tricks, and desertions, she had grown a little cynical. Now here she was, telling herself that all she wanted was to be with this man.

They were shown to a table in a secluded corner, where green candles rose from posies of fresh white flowers.

'You're spoiling me,' whispered Bethan, loving it.

When the meal was almost over, Ray said, 'I missed you last weekend.'

Bethan carefully laid her fork down.

'I missed you too.'

'Couldn't you have got away?'

'I—could have done. I wasn't sure—'

She didn't want to bring any note of disharmony into this perfect evening.

'I know I upset you that day. The fact is, you completely numbed me, saying you were going to learn to fly.'

'I don't understand.'

'You'd need to know a lot more about me to do that. I was married, as you've probably gathered. Trixie and I knew each other from our teens. We had everything going for us, but somehow, it was never right.'

This is going to be painful, thought Bethan with sympathy. But she kept silent.

'We battled through the early years, but as things got worse she grew wilder. Off for months, without a word. Travelling in India and Khatmandu. Dossing down in London

65

with down-and-outs. Underwater diving in the Red Sea. Anything for sensation. Something drove her all the time. The boys couldn't hold her, and I certainly couldn't.'

The grey shades of past unhappiness were gathered in his face.

'If you'd rather not tell me,' said Bethan quietly.

'I'd rather tell you. We both knew we were at crisis point. We were getting a divorce, when she came back, and announced that she'd stay here with us, and learn to fly. Richard thought she was wonderful. She terrified Tom. He never knew how to take her.'

Ray paused regretfully, then continued.

'He used to hide from her. One day he did it, and she was furious. She flung out of the house and went down to the airfield. She took up a plane without anyone's permission. She crashed it, and killed herself.'

'Oh, my dear.' Bethan reached for Ray's hand.

'I did love her—once.'

There was the bleakness of former sorrow in his voice.

'So when you said you were going to learn to fly—'

'I understand,' said Bethan, and meant it. 'But I'm not Trixie. I'm a city girl, who's suddenly woken up to all I was missing. And flying fascinates me. You started me off,

66

showing me that picture of wartime pilot David Blake.'

'If I lost you now—'

'You won't,' said Bethan with conviction. 'That's the last thing I intend to happen. I shall play it by the book. And in future I intend to avoid that derelict air camp at night.'

'Why do you say that?'

'After the barbeque, I thought you were angry with me. I was walking there when it was getting dark.'

'On your own?'

She nodded and continued. 'I can see more pretty weird people hang around there. I bumped into an airman, who asked me the way.'

'You *what?*'

'He looked pretty ropy—torn clothes; in fact, I thought they were bloodstained. He had such a desperate look about him, I wondered if he was drunk.'

'Bethan. For heaven's sake.'

Ray had a look of mingled concern and incredulity.

'What's the matter?'

'You certainly will have to promise me not to go wandering around there on your own. Someone ought to have warned you. That was the ghost of Linwell Johnny.'

CHAPTER SEVEN

Bethan gazed at him in disbelief as the words sank in.

'But—what are you talking about?'

Ray squeezed her hand. He was warm, and strong, and reassuring.

'Cheer up. It will probably never happen again. But it's a bit of a local legend. Ever since the war, people have recounted seeing Linwell Johnny, a lost airman in bloodstained flying-gear who pleaded to find the way home.'

A delicate shiver ran along Bethan's spine. This evening was proving surprising in more ways than one.

'D'you think I'm fated?' she asked, feigning light-heartedness, for there was still a small shadow hovering.

'I think you're beautiful. And you came into my life when I badly needed you.'

How could she not be happy when he spoke with such sincerity? The small misunderstanding that had arisen had blown away like feathers in the wind.

'Then I'm truly happy,' she said. If there had been shadows over this evening, the ghost of Trixie, and the ghost of a lonely, lost airman, then surely two living, flesh-and-blood people could exorcise them, sharing a future that was bright and secure?

As they drank delicious coffee, Ray outlined his plan for tomorrow—picking up the boys in the morning, collecting Bethan, then driving to a local safari and adventure park for a picnic.

They sat chatting easily until most of the other diners had left, then Ray drove Bethan back to the cottage, where they lingered in the fragrant summer darkness, loath to break the spell. A bedroom curtain in one of the cottages twitched. Bethan laughed.

'Goodbye, Ray,' she said reluctantly, longing with all her heart for some bright day when they would not have to say goodbye. The walls of the cottage closed around her, familiar and comforting. She thought of the absent Maggie, and murmured a small thank-you for a place that had already become a cornerstone in her life.

She was up early, not willing to admit to the slight nerves she felt at meeting Ray's sons. When Bethan thought of it calmly, it seemed ludicrous that a woman whose job was to handle celebrities of various types should have qualms about two small boys.

But today might be crucial. If they didn't like her, Ray might have second thoughts about his continuing relationship with Bethan. And if anything did go wrong, she couldn't bear it.

Telling herself not to be so anxious, she considered what to wear; then a bit of ordinary devil-may-care reasserted itself, and she dressed brightly in jeans and a white and yellow checked shirt, adding jaunty ear-rings to complete the picture. The car arrived. Ray tooted his horn, and Bethan ran down the path.

Impeccably mannered, as always, Ray held the front passenger-seat door open for her, then said, 'Bethan, this is Richard and Tom.'

The older boy, dark-haired, bony, did not lift his eyes from the book he was reading. The youngest boy, Tom, his fair hair an unruly tangle, regarded her warily, his uncertainty written plain on his honest little face.

'Hi,' said Bethan, determined to be casual.

'Hi,' croaked Tom, a hectic blush spreading over his skin. Richard was silent.

Ray turned the radio to a pop-music channel, and they drove with no more conversation. Bethan tried to sort out her feelings. Being with Ray was good, but this way it was different. Previously it had been Ray, the single man, the potential lover, the pursuer and the hunter. Now this was Ray the father, cautious and caring. For a bleak moment, Bethan felt like an outsider.

They reached their destination, and parked by a children's area, where people could wander around. As soon as the car stopped, Richard sprang out, and hared away.

'It's all right,' said Ray, taking in Bethan's look of alarm. 'He's heading for the reptile house. He won't go anywhere else.'

'Can we see the rabbits? Can we see the rabbits?' Tom was jumping up and down.

'Rabbits ahoy,' agreed Bethan briskly, marching off, military style, in the direction of an arrow on a signboard.

'Do that again. Do that again.' Tom was gurgling with amusement. He hopped alongside Bethan.

'What?' she asked.

'You know. Like soldiers.'

'Right, sir. Like this, sir?'

This seemed to be an uncomplicated little soul, thought Bethan. It was the other one who might prove more difficult. They strolled around looking at a variety of small animals, then reached a lake, where downy ducklings could be fed from paper bags full of seed. Small balls of fluff bombed about on the water, squeaking as they searched for titbits. The mother duck hovered near.

'Where's their dad?' asked Tom, muddy and pond-stained.

'He'll be around,' replied Ray.

'Probably left them or got eaten by a fox.'

'There he is,' said Bethan, spotting a handsome mallard with a turquoise head. Somehow she didn't want this conversation to stay downbeat.

They were to eat a picnic lunch, then drive through the rest of the park, which had strong fences and gates because of dangerous animals allowed to roam freely.

Richard came back, and they spread a car-rug on the grass. The older boy ate in silence, answering only in monosyllables. When the others were clearing up, he went to sit alone by the pond.

Bethan sent a questioning look to Ray. Leave him, said his eyes. She nodded.

They drove through the rest of the park with windows closed, not stopping, catching glimpses of prides of lions, and lean, grey wolves that glared their hatred from their hillocks and caves. Giraffe regarded them haughtily, and plump zebra trotted across the track. It was all innocent fun, except for one ten-year-old boy, who shrouded himself in his own cocoon.

On the drive back to Southbeck, Tom fell asleep. When they reached Bethan's cottage, he awoke with a jerk.

'Don't go,' he pleaded, his face still flushed with slumber. 'I don't want you to go.'

But the boys had to be driven back to their school premises, and Ray would be occupied for some time yet.

'There'll be another time,' she replied, resisting an impulse to hug this small, muddy person, not because she did not want to, but because it might cause resentment in the other child.

72

'Soon,' said Ray firmly.

Bethan went indoors, trying not to think of the long evening hours still to be filled. It all seemed a bit pointless without Ray, yet if she was to be a permanent part of his life there would be many times when she had to share him with others.

It was almost midnight, and she was sitting in a pretty pink robe, her hair tousled, her skin rosy from a bath, when he came back. She didn't need to ask who was at the door, for no one else in Southbeck would call at this time. He walked straight in, and gathered her into his arms, kissing her hungrily, as though they had been apart for months. Laughing and breathless, Bethan pushed him away.

'Did I pass the test?' she asked lightly.

'It was a good day,' Ray said firmly. 'They liked you.'

'Both of them?'

'Tom thought you were wonderful.'

'And Richard?'

'He's more cautious. You've got to give him time, Bethan. He's still bleeding for Trixie. But all wounds heal in the end.'

He drew her back into his arms, and there was a new urgency in him, an impatience, a stronger, rising current of desire.

'You're very desirable,' he whispered, and somehow, the pink robe fell to the floor, and she could feel the slog-slog of his heart, heavy

73

and jerky under his thin shirt.

All the pent-up longing of years rose inside her, welling out towards him in a yearning for that full and consummated love that would bond them together in a way that no one could sever.

A true and lasting relationship, built on honour and trust. It would have been easy to let him stay the night, bliss for both of them, but it was worth more than that.

'Ray,' she said gently. 'Richard needs time. So do I.'

She felt disappointment empty through him. He slackened, then sighed.

'Love you, Bethan,' he said simply. Tears sprang into her eyes, for he had touched her deeply, and she half wondered if it would not have been simpler just to let nature win. We have something going for us, he had said. They had, and it was too precious to squander.

Already it was the early hours of Monday morning, and a workaday week lay ahead. At this point, Harvey Lime and his London background seemed almost as far away as the planet Mars.

'Next weekend's going to be hectic,' said Ray apologetically. 'The boys will be home for the summer, and then we have our big demo coming up. I'm afraid there's going to be some trouble, but we're not backing down now.'

'Trouble?' echoed Bethan.

'This stand-up fight of ours has gained quite a lot of publicity, which of course we welcome, except that it usually attracts a loony crowd who come to stir up mischief. We shall have newsmen and TV cameras all looking for a shindig, and very disappointed if they don't find it.'

By now, Ray was sprawled easily on the settee. He looked tired, but with the light of determination in his eyes.

'When's the big day?' she asked.

'Officially, Wednesday, July 7th, but we believe that's a tale to mislead us—so they can move in before we're ready. We've got a reliable source that tells us they'll move in, dig and dump before then—to beat us.'

'That's mean,' said Bethan indignantly.

'They'd call it strategy. But we shall be ready. You've heard of sieges in days gone by, to keep out the enemy. That's what Southbeck will be like.'

Up to now, Bethan had only had a marginal interest in village warfare against the dumpers, wholly because of Ray. But things had changed. From being a village she didn't know existed, Southbeck had become important as the scene of her future happiness. She didn't care for politics, but she did care for health, and peace, and freedom. Weren't those the things that flyers like David Blake had been fighting for?

When Ray had gone, she snatched a few

75

hours sleep, then left for London, preparing for a busy week. Mark Lime was very much in evidence, and straws in the wind told Bethan that he was planning a future take-over.

She tidied up what odds and ends she could, and told Mark that next week she would be taking a few days off. His reaction was non-committal. It confirmed her own view that his business methods would be different, and that he wouldn't mind too much about loosening strings with the past.

The weekend seemed a long time coming. Bethan visited Harvey, who was now at home for a spell, awaiting a return visit to hospital for his bypass surgery. She found him in a mood of gloom, that spread around him like a damp fog.

He listened gloomily, whilst she outlined what had happened with various contracts and agreements, skating over problems. No doubt he had already heard this from Mark. Or did Mark prefer to work unencumbered?

Whilst Mary fluttered around with coffee-cups, Harvey picked at a biscuit, the epitome of a man with the meaning taken out of his life.

'I suppose you'll be going next,' he said huffily to Bethan.

'Not yet,' she replied, sorry for his troubles, which seemed like a river bearing him downstream.

He had been good to her, and she would give

him what loyalty she could. All the same, she couldn't help feeling that with Mark Lime at the helm, there wouldn't be much room for either Harvey or Bethan.

She drove to Southbeck on Friday evening, wondering how different it was going to be with Ray's sons around. A quarter of a mile from the village, she slowed. Posters draped the hedgerows, and half a dozen farm tractors, some old and decrepit, blocked the road. A bald wooden sign, daubed in angry red, announced *This village is closed.*

Nonplussed, Bethan got out. Even a tank couldn't have got past there.

Half a dozen youths were busily employed closing up a gap in the hedge with rolls of barbed wire. An older man was directing operations.

Helplessly, Bethan stood watching. The man came over.

'Sorry,' he said. He sounded firm, and not particularly apologetic.

'I've got to get into Southbeck,' she said. 'There's a cottage where I stay.'

He studied her solemnly.

'If you go back about a mile to Petersons' farm, they'll let you use a track. It comes out behind the church. It's rough, but just about driveable. That'll be blocked up before tomorrow.'

Bethan thanked him and left. He was right,

77

the track was rough, and she shuddered for the car's suspension. Arriving at the cottage, she discovered the neighbours, in a group, on the grass. The woman from the middle cottage beckoned her over.

'Maybe you ought to know, the village hall is headquarters, and there'll be teams on duty round the clock. We don't reckon there'll be much doing tomorrow, but after that—it's any time. When they get here, we'll be ready for 'em.'

She grinned at Bethan conspiratorially.

'All right, isn't it?'

The woman's eyes gleamed. There was something in her face suggesting that if it was a fight they were looking for, she would be ready.

Inside the cottage, there was a bowl of fresh flowers on the table, and a note from Ray. The barmaid at the inn hadn't mentioned that he had borrowed the key, but why should she? The note said 'It's all systems go, but the village hall will know where to find me. Love you. Ray.'

Bemused by these events, Bethan went to bed. She was part of Southbeck now, to some tune. No doubt the other road end, in or out of the village, was sealed. Like it or not, she was living under siege.

CHAPTER EIGHT

Morning brought dismal skies, and shoals of rain. Dismayed, Bethan peered through the cottage window. No life showed at the other houses, where gardens were muddy pools, and Brussels sprouts running amok rose dripping craggily like tortured stalagmites.

Uncertain how to tackle the day, Bethan remembered Ray's note, and the fact that he could be contacted at the village hall. Mid-morning, she donned a roomy cagoule, which hung in the cottage kitchen, and set off through the rain.

As she splashed her way along, various heavy farm-type vehicles passed in a convoy, loaded with bales of straw, horse-jumping stands, and all manner of other things for further road obstruction. The faces of the men in the driving seats were not uncheerful, but they had the look of those who would brook no nonsense.

Bethan shivered as the rain ran down her face. Southbeck was closed. She was here now, and unless she wanted to walk out, here she would stay.

The village hall hummed with activity. On a trestle-table in one corner, women were cutting up sandwiches and serving coffee. Children ran about, restraint thrown off, because there was the urgent feeling of a looming crisis. Everybody wore a black and white rosette, with the words *Southbeck Says No*. Several teenagers were costumed in long white shrouds, with skull and crossbones painted in black on the front.

Scanning the room, Bethan saw no sign of Ray, but at the far end a few children were sitting around a table with crayons and jigsaw puzzles. Tom Allington spotted her, his face breaking into a smile. Bethan went over.

'Hi,' she said. 'What's new?'

'Nothing.' Tom scowled. 'It's boring.'

'Sit down,' ordered Richard, without looking up. Acting as older brother was serious to him.

For want of anything better to do, Bethan pulled up a chair. A small, grubby boy, who looked as though his hair hadn't seen a brush inside a month, passed her his drawing for approval. Gravely examining a purple cow in a pea-green field, Bethan murmured words of encouragement, then her eyes fixed on what Richard was doing.

In front of him was a large sheet of paper, which he had covered with grotesque shapes of black trees. Lurid orange and yellow flames leapt up like the panting tongues of savage animals. A dress torn into holes drooped from one tree. Part of an arm was lodged in another. Long brown hair fluttered from a twisted branch.

Bethan hid her dismay, appalled at the distress so innocently revealed. Her hand reached out, and covered Richard's in sympathy. He did not meet her eyes, but there was a moment before he drew his hand away.

By lunch-time, various groups of dripping-wet men drifted in, whilst the trestle-table ladies served hot soup. Ray came in with Trash Morgan, and both his boys immediately made a dash for their father. Trash acknowledged Bethan with a tight smile that was neither friendly nor unfriendly.

Ray came over to Bethan and said, 'Look, I'm sorry, this is probably not much fun for you, but we're not sure when the trucks will be here, and we can't let up. It won't be long. That we know.'

He gave her a smile that made everyone and everything else vanish, and suddenly it didn't matter, not even if she had to stay here for a week.

'What's happening?' she asked.

'It's pretty hectic out there. All sorts of people have turned up at the road-blocks: genuine supporters, men selling hamburgers, hippies with peace banners, those who just came to stare. The police are doing a good job, but if the rain lets up, it's going to get worse.'

They shared hot soup with the children, and the day dragged on. Towards late afternoon the rain cleared, and young limbs that had been constrained burst out into fresh air and freedom. A message came that a television camera crew had arrived at one road-block, and people started out for there, wishing to taste the excitement.

Taking charge of Richard and Tom, Bethan gazed in astonishment at the heaving mass of humanity on the outside of the road barrier. The air was loud with voices, transistor radios, the boom of a loudhailer as the police strove to keep order.

Tents had been set up on grass verges, people were boiling kettles on picnic stoves, some had hung out strings of wet clothes to dry. For the first time, Bethan felt a chill of fear. Until this moment, her mind had not contemplated the realities of the clash. She had certainly not been prepared for such hordes of people, many of them not from Southbeck, but drawn to the scene by the promise of trouble, even violence.

Towering head and shoulders above the other women, Bethan saw the shaggy, blonde head of Julie, the girl she had met at the barbeque. With relief, Bethan headed towards her, the boys in tow, grateful for a familiar face in the mob.

Julie hailed her cheerfully, saying, 'More hands, light work,' then gave the boys black plastic sacks, and told them to go round picking up the litter.

'This is a peaceful demonstration,' she said

firmly. 'We want to keep our village beautiful, not wreck it.'

Their attention was drawn to a mild commotion outside the barrier, as television cameramen tried to move forward to speak with bona fide villagers. Drowning the voice of the spokesman, a hippie with a guitar broke in with a song about revolution.

By evening, Bethan's head was aching. The children's faces looked tired, their eyes were dark in sunken sockets. Ray, who had come and gone all afternoon, said to Bethan, 'Nothing's going to happen before midnight. There are camp-beds set up in the village hall. Would you take the boys there?'

Wearily, they trudged back. An atmosphere of bonhomie still prevailed, the kind of spirit Bethan imagined had been common during the war. She sent the two boys into a cloakroom to wash their dirty hands and faces, then sat in a canvas chair between two makeshift beds. For Tom and Richard, oblivion came within minutes.

The place quietened down. Bethan dozed, fighting off sleep that threatened to engulf her. It had been an odd sort of day. She opened her eyes at one point to see Trash Morgan standing at the end of Tom's bed, an expression she didn't know on his face. She had caught him off his guard. The moment he felt Bethan's eyes on him, Morgan turned and strode away.

In between snatches of sleep, she wondered blearily what was happening out there. People tossed and shuffled on the primitive camp-beds, mostly children. In the hall, a handful of adults still kept vigil. The night took on the raw feeling of aching emptiness.

She awoke abruptly, coming back from a pleasant dream, where she and Ray had been drifting in a boat on the river. A man she recognised as the innkeeper stood looking down at her.

'Things are moving,' he informed her gruffly. 'Maybe you want to come, or maybe you want to stay here. Please yourself. But if you want to come with us, Jake's in charge here. He doesn't want to be involved in anything that might gain him publicity.' No, thought Bethan, with a flash of the old antipathy. Jake wants a lot of things, but sometimes he doesn't know what they are.

Her next reaction was that she should back up Ray. He was in this up to the hilt, a hundred per cent committed, not hedging his bets, and juggling alternatives.

She pulled on the cagoule, and made her way into the hall. A few people stood talking, an undercurrent of excitement in their voices. Morgan stood with them, even in a group looking a solitary figure. Bethan glanced at her watch. It was one o'clock in the morning.

'What's happening then?' she asked.

The local vicar, a tall, spare man, with a domed bald head, answered. 'We got word from a town forty miles away that there's a whole convoy of trucks on the way. They know about our roadblocks. Most of the country knows by now, and our mole thinks the trucks could try to force a way over farm-land and open country.'

Bethan stared.

'Can they do that?'

'Evidently—if we let them. If we hadn't been tipped off, they'd have been in here, and had the job done under the cover of darkness, and away again, before we could stop them.'

I don't like it, she told herself starkly. The politics of this I am content to leave to others. But in there sleep innocent children who trust us. We must deserve that trust.

Outside, a large crowd was getting ready to move, more than a hundred people. Most of them held torches, or lights of some kind. In the darkness, the flickering lights lit up their faces, which were grim with determination.

A group gathered around Ray listened intently as he outlined the plan.

'We know they've got to reach Pond Acre—that's the site chosen by the Ministry. What we've got to do is stop them. There's roughly only one area where they can try their approach, otherwise they're stopped by dykes and a river. That's Porritt's farmland. Poor old chap. He's nearly eighty, and that farm's been his life.'

Whatever old Porritt thought about it, he was in for a shock, reflected Bethan, as she walked beside Ray. Somebody nearby expressed the hope that Porritt's son would have got him out of it, and another gloomy voice came back with the answer that how the hell could he, as nobody knew until now, and in any case, old Porritt hadn't budged off the place in twenty years.

Silence fell over the shuffling army. Someone started whistling, but a woman's voice sharply bade the whistler be silent. Everyone moved with speed and urgency. Behind her, Bethan could hear the bronchial breathing of an old man struggling to keep up.

The outbuildings of Porritt's farm came into view, crouching like great, sleeping creatures in the blackness around. The house was in darkness. Ray had told Bethan than an attempt had been made to warn the household by telephone, but no one had answered.

A halt was called, and a man was delegated to go and bang on the farmhouse door, to alert the occupants as to what was going on.

Presently a light appeared at an upstairs window, and messages were shouted two or three times before the old man caught on. Moments elapsed, and he appeared again in the window with a shotgun.

'He won't need that,' said Ray quietly. 'It's not rabbits we're after.'

'God almighty!' The startled blasphemy fell chill on Bethan's ears as a convoy of trucks appeared half a mile away, their brilliant headlights slicing the darkness. Ray drew in a sharp breath.

'They're coming. They've only got two possible ways, through the farmyard, or down at the end and over the potato fields. I'll keep a dozen people here with me by the farm. Harold and Reg, take charge of the rest, and move down to that end. Make a line, block them with bodies, just block them any way you can.'

Bethan shivered, vowing to keep close to Ray, whose contingent was already moving into place. Steadily mowing down fences, flattening crops, the great ugly trucks moved nearer.

Furious now with this invasion of his property, old Porritt fired off a couple of shots into the air. It was answered by the shrill screeching of pigs, agitated and fearful at the commotion.

The trucks were heading for the gap between the farm and outbuildings. Bethan felt herself tremble. A panic-edged sense of approaching doom welded the protestors into a solid phalanx of obstruction. The first truck halted, the others followed suit. The driver, a youngish man in regulation protective clothing got down and shouted, 'Let us pass!'

Ray told his supporters to say nothing, not to be provoked. But there was no need. Another volley of shots rang out as old Porritt screamed, 'Get off my property! This is my land. Get off, or I'll 'ave yer, the lot of yer!'

Breathless, choking, the little band stood unmoving.

'I'm coming down,' shouted Porritt. 'There's me bull in the barn. 'E'll 'av yer. This is private property, private, d'you hear?'

He slammed the window closed, and downstairs lights went on. The truck-driver signalled to his mate, and got back in the cab. Painstakingly, the line reversed, making for another approach at the end.

Bethan leaned against Ray, thinking how much she would like to sit down, but various members of their group showed signs of wanting to run to the others.

'We must stay here,' advised Ray. 'Leave no gaps. We mustn't weaken.'

Porritt came out, an ancient overcoat over his pyjamas. The immediate threat having been averted, he grinned. He had not had time to put in his teeth, and the threat about the bull seemed to be forgotten.

'Is that it?' asked Bethan shakily.

'I shouldn't think so,' said Ray. 'They'll have their man from the Ministry to tell us we've obstructed the law, and so on. We just hold on—say nothing.'

Old Porritt, who moved in a series of stringy jerks, seemed to have been injected with new life. He retreated into the kitchen and made mugs of tea, handing them round, bubbling away about his farm, his son, who was never there when he was wanted, off running after some no-good woman or other, no use to his old dad. The old boy had spirit, thought Bethan, gratefully sipping the tea.

Keeping his stalwart body of protestors together, Ray moved them a short distance so that they could have a better view of what was going on. In the darkness, the torches of the other Southbeck folk glimmered eerily as they formed a barrier two deep.

The trucks were halted, and carrying in the stillness Bethan could hear the angry shouts of the drivers as they tried to jeer the villagers out of the way. No one moved. No one spoke or replied to the hurled abuse.

It was an impasse. Weary with the day's events, someone in front of the trucks sat down upon the ground. In ones and twos, others did the same. With this simple act, they gave the impression of being prepared to stay there indefinitely.

Dawn was streaking the sky as the silent truck-drivers returned to their cabins and drove away. Still the villagers held on. When eventually a message came through on Porritt's telephone to say that the trucks had been seen leaving the area, only then did the protestors leave.

Tired but triumphant, some drifted off for home, others headed for the village hall. Bethan, followed by Ray, went to look for the boys. Richard sat on his camp-bed, reading. Tom's bed was empty.

CHAPTER NINE

'Where's Tom?' asked Ray cheerfully. A small warning bell tolled in Bethan's brain. Silly, she told herself. You're just tired. Or the child has gone to the toilet. Or to play somewhere else.

'I don't know.' Richard seldom spoke more than a few words.

'Explain please.' Ray's voice had sharpened.

'I told you. I don't know.' The boy's tone had taken on the edge of someone accused of falling down in his duty. 'When I woke up, he wasn't here. I've asked around, but nobody's seen him.'

Bethan could see Ray weighing this up, sorting out the possibilities, and deciding it was nothing to worry about. Certainly, nothing that should be allowed to trouble Richard.

'Okay,' said Ray soothing, 'I expect he's around. You stay here, do you understand? Don't move from here.'

He went back into the main room, leaving Bethan looking down on the head of the ten-year-old boy. Richard projected the image of a child that didn't care, but Bethan suspected that was far from true. She sat down on Tom's bed, her hands clasped in front of her. She felt tired and dirty, and suddenly, in these last moments, an outsider.

'He was always doing that,' said Richard, in a voice so low Bethan scarcely caught the words.

'Doing what?' she asked, hoping the question wouldn't break the frail thread of communication.

'Running off and hiding. He did it when Mum was there. She used to go crazy, hunting up and down for him. You might think I should stop him, but I can't. How can I when I don't know?'

'You can't,' replied Bethan. 'You're not to worry. He'll be around.'

'He was there when I went to sleep.' The boy rambled on as though Bethan hadn't spoken. 'I woke up once or twice, when Jake was standing by the bed, but I didn't look at Tom. Why should I?'

'Let's get something to eat,' Bethan decided. The delectable smell of bacon sandwiches was teasing her nose. She was hungry, almost sleep-walking, and a nasty maggot of doubt was beginning to gnaw in her mind. Maybe she was to blame. Maybe she shouldn't have left the village hall.

She went out into the main room where mugs of tea and sandwiches were being passed around. The general mood seemed to be one of elation, for the dumpers had been routed, at least for the present. Only Ray looked preoccupied, and when Bethan joined him, she knew at once that no one had seen Tom.

Some silent message that flashed between them told Bethan to play this low-key for now.

'We've checked the hall, and the yard outside,' said Ray quietly. 'It's possible he's scampered off with some other children. The trouble is, people have been going and coming all night. It's hard to pin anyone down.'

'Where is Morgan?' asked Bethan, sharply remembering. Her voice caught the attention of a woman in a nylon overall, who replied, 'He went home when the news came through that the dumpers had gone away.'

And that was hours ago, thought Bethan bleakly. Had Morgan just shelved responsibility? It was a thing in which he had some experience.

'There's been a team on all the time.' The woman paused with the loaded tray, providing Morgan with an alibi, like impressionable females often sprang to do.

'He was telling Tom a story.' This came from a grandmotherly type, for others were listening now.

92

'What time?' asked Ray.

The grandmother shrugged. So much happened, she implied.

Needles of panic were beginning to stab Bethan. What sort of a mess was this she had landed them all in? Where *was* Tom? Morgan appeared to be the last person who had seen him. Wasn't there something odd about Morgan, and the way he had stood looking down at those sleeping children? Could Tom have gone with him?

'Ray,' she said, touching his arm. 'Telephone Morgan. He might know.'

Ray nodded briefly, and strode off to make the call. Five minutes later he was back.

'Jake isn't there,' he said. 'His housekeeper answered. He got home this morning, had a shower, and left for the airfield. He had a private plane booked to fly him to London.'

'Did you ask if Tom was with him?' asked Bethan, her voice edged with broken glass.

'Yes I did. The housekeeper was still in bed when Jake came in, but she knew he was flying to London, so she didn't take much notice, and she didn't see him at all.'

By now, most people knew something was wrong, and that this cast a shadow on former jubilation. Bethan glanced anxiously at Ray, whose face was tinged with a greyness that was more than weariness. One man, then another, volunteered to organise a group to go out into the village, knocking on doors, searching outbuildings and garden huts, looking in every possible place for the missing child. In the bustle of their departure, Bethan felt a hand on her sleeve.

'I'm hungry,' whispered Richard.

'Sorry,' she whispered in return, ashamed at having forgotten his needs and his feelings. She brought sandwiches and warm drinks; then as they ate, she realised how much she needed this help, to stop her whole body from trembling.

Richard ate so ravenously that Bethan once more felt a twinge of guilt. These children had been involved in something that was adult business; yesterday had been long and erratic, with skimpy and irregular meals. Sitting here with this different boy, who always seemed to be on the edge of everything, Bethan felt the stirrings of empathy. It couldn't be expressed in words, because that would embarrass Richard acutely, but at least she could share these moments.

'They'll find him,' she assured the boy, lightly touching his shoulder.

'Will they?' He stared at her, and in the moment before his eyes fell, she saw the absolute naked fear and misery. 'Tom's always been Dad's favourite. If anything happens to Tom—'

'It won't,' said Bethan, with more conviction than she felt.

It looked like being the sort of day that again would be totally unpredictable, a lot of hanging about and wondering what was going to happen next. The temptation to creep away home and crawl into bed was very strong, but there was no chance of that, not with one child unaccounted for, and another on his own here.

At lunch-time, the search-parties came back, reporting no success. By now, most people in Southbeck knew that eight-year-old Tom Allington was missing, the police had been informed, and a local radio station was putting out the story.

After the heady excitement of yesterday, when the dumpers had been challenged and defeated, today seemed a cruel and bitter anticlimax. Watching Ray, whose face was haggard as he pushed a sandwich aside uneaten, Bethan felt helpless with misery. She wanted to help, and yet there was nothing she could do.

'What now?' she asked him, her voice unsteady.

'The police are mounting a search, combing fields and woods, and there's some talk of dragging the river.'

'Oh.' Colour drained from Bethan's face. Even the idea of poor little Tom helpless in the water turned her bones to jelly. This whole thing was running wild like a nightmare.

'Look,' said Bethan, desperately clutching at any straw. 'The last person who saw him was

Morgan. Where *is* Morgan? Why can't he be contacted?'

'He can't,' replied Ray resignedly. 'We've tried his housekeeper again, and all she knows is he's gone to London. She asked him when he'd be back, and he couldn't say. I got the impression he didn't want to tell her much about it.'

'She'll be used to that,' Bethan added bitterly. 'Morgan doesn't like being tied down to times and arrangements. I should know.'

Ray smiled.

'Could he have taken Tom with him?' asked Bethan.

'Why should he do that?'

'I don't know, but I don't understand a lot of what Morgan does. You said yourself the boys went to him like lambs. That Morgan likes children. Maybe he had some impulse that overpowered him.'

'To take Tom away?' Ray stared at her, thunderstruck. 'D'you mean—abduct the child?'

Bethan laughed harshly.

'Morgan makes his own rules. He told me he was tired of the glitz, and only wanted a quiet life. He has a child of his own, although he's only just beginning to acknowledge it. Maybe he's got his thinking twisted.'

By afternoon, most people had drifted away in search of rest and relief. The road-blocks had been cleared, and although Southbeck was now a spot in the national news, things were grinding back to normal. Ray suggested that the three of them returned to Wood Hall for a few hours sleep.

But in spite of the beautiful guest-room, which was furnished in soft shades of creamy white and pink, Bethan could only doze, her nerves too taut for rest.

Ray slept, and so did his son. Forlorn with worry, Bethan switched on the television set, to catch the news. After international headlines, then national events, a picture of the police in waders dragging a dyke flashed on the screen, with the words *Southbeck Siege. Boy Vanishes.*

Sick at heart, she killed the picture, wondering why one family's torment should be a titbit for the rest of the gawping world. In her present mood, there was only anger, and grey despair.

The house was still quiet, as Ray and the boy slept on. Bethan did not grudge them a few hours of oblivion, but the sense of utter loneliness filled her again. The waiting was unbearable, all these hours, not knowing whether Tom was alive or dead, longing for news, and almost dreading what it would be when it came.

Ray woke about six o'clock, showered, and went down to the kitchen to get a meal together. Barely speaking, Bethan helped where she could. Her hands felt clumsy, her legs leaden. There was so much she wanted to pour out to Ray, to tell him she understood the depths of his fears, but no words would come. A bleary-eyed Richard had come downstairs to join them when the telephone rang. Ray came back from answering, and Bethan could tell from his face that nothing had changed for the better.

'Who was it?' she croaked.

'Perc. Captain Harris from the Air Club. The news about Tom has only just caught up with him.'

'Oh,' said Bethan tightly.

'He was at the club this morning when Jake left. Jake was on his own. No sign of Tom.'

Another door closed, thought Bethan bleakly. It had been a long shot, but if there had been anything in it, and if, for some erratic reason best known to himself, Morgan had taken Tom away, at least they would have known the boy was alive and well.

The three of them sat down at the table, although Bethan felt food would choke her. But the two males ate, and in a few minutes Richard said shyly, 'This is nice.'

Ray, whose mind was miles away, said, 'What is?'

'Sitting here, like a family.'

Clouds like thunder gathered on Ray's brow.

'That's a stupid statement,' he said bitingly.

'One member of this family is missing, we don't know where. This is no family until Tom comes back.'

Painful colour spread over Richard's sallow face at the rebuke. Bethan's heart ached for him, a ten-year-old boy caught in adult cross-currents he did not understand. In this, she and Richard were allies, pushed by circumstances into a position they were powerless to change.

Ray got up and went out. The study door slammed, but from the faint murmur of his voice, Bethan knew he was making telephone calls, clutching at straws, anything to ease the pain of waiting.

Bethan reached across the table, and brushed Richard's hand. She could see him struggling to hold back the tears.

'Don't be upset,' she implored him. 'When grown-ups are worried, they often say cruel and thoughtless things.'

The boy bit his lip. He worshipped his mother, thought Bethan, slicing through to the core of it. He worshipped her, and he lost her. Now Tom has gone. How much more can one small boy take?

Although she hadn't mothered the child, his helpless grief seeped through to her.

'Tom will be all right.' She spoke with such strength that Richard stared at her.

'How d'you know?'

'Because you said he was always running off, always hiding. He never came to harm, did he? Tom's a survivor. He'll be all right. You see.'

Ray returned, no anger left in his face, but no relief either.

'I can't bear waiting any longer,' he said gruffly. 'Let's get out in the car, tour around, see what's going on. I feel so helpless just waiting here.'

It was a relief to be moving, thought Bethan, grateful for action of any kind. She was feeling marginally better. Her own words to Richard had convinced herself as well. Tom was bright as sunshine, a strong, lusty child with his own definite ideas. He was as sharp as a box of razorblades.

They drove around the village, where the home-made banners and placards still fluttered in defiance, then out along roads and lanes, seeing in some places the evidences of police searchers at work, still meticulously combing each inch of ground.

Then they drew up at the local police-station, where an officer came out to speak to Ray.

'No news yet, sir.' The man's face betrayed nothing. 'Best go home and wait, sir. We'll let you know as soon as there's any news.'

There seemed nothing else to do but comply. When Ray ran his car onto the drive at Wood Hall, a truck followed. As Ray, Bethan and Richard climbed out, the truck door slammed.

100

Morgan strolled forward.

'Where've you been, Jake?' asked Ray, unsmiling. 'We've been trying to talk to you all day.'

'Well now, that's interesting,' drawled Morgan, having instantly picked up the tension in Ray, and putting up his defence of casualness, 'because I've been trying to telephone you and getting nowhere.'

Ray's face lightened the first time in hours. 'About Tom?'

Morgan's eyebrows shot up.

'Tom? No. I wanted to get hold of Bethan, and she seems to be your constant companion.'

'You don't know anything about Tom?' burst out Bethan, on hot bricks at this studied exchange.

'Not a thing,' replied Morgan. 'Should I?'

'But when you flew off to London—'

'I went to pick up Alys from Heathrow,' interrupted Morgan. 'She flew in from Vancouver. She's back at Dyke Farm with Dan. I thought you'd like to know.'

CHAPTER TEN

Ray's shoulders sagged again, the only fact important to him being that there was no good news about Tom. Bethan struggled with this new piece of information. She stared at Morgan, trying to put words together.

'Let me get this straight. Alys came back from Vancouver? You went to meet her, and you brought her here?'

Morgan nodded.

'She's tired. It's a long flight, and she needs to sleep. But I thought you ought to know.'

'Trust you, Morgan,' said Bethan, the old bitterness welling up. 'You always made your own rules. Alys had a new life. Why couldn't you—?'

'It's between Alys and me, surely?' Morgan half smiled, his voice painstakingly patient. 'I telephoned and told her I wanted her back. We've a lot to talk about.'

Added to the nightmare of Tom's disappearance, all the old anguish was being stirred up again. Bethan felt the smart of tears behind her eyes.

'So you don't know about Tom?' This was Ray, urgent to bring the main matter back. Before Morgan could reply, Richard burst in with 'Tom's missing, and it's all my fault.'

'No,' said Bethan, vexed that the boy should have been pushed so far.

'It is, it is.'

Tears rained down Richard's face.

Bethan fumbled for a handkerchief, but it was Morgan who drew the shaking figure of the boy into his arms.

'Now this won't do,' he comforted. 'How could anyone blame a splendid brother like you? Haven't I seen all the ways you look after Tom, whenever you can?'

Richard's sobs subsided a little, and Morgan, looking directly at Ray, said, 'On the way here, I saw some police activity, but I assumed it was still something to do with the demo. Then I stopped for petrol at a service-station, and the attendant said something about a little lad who had gone missing. But he mentioned no names, and I never dreamed it was anyone I knew.'

Richard had quietened down, and Ray patted his head, telling him not to be such a silly goose. The bubble of the child's guilt had been pricked. If only the telephone would ring, yearned Bethan. If only.

'Is there anything I can do?' asked Morgan. 'Anything at all?'

'Yes,' said Ray quietly. 'Go back to Dyke Farm. You've enough on your mind. Everything that can be done is being done. Thank you for coming and letting us know.'

I won't think about it, Bethan told herself, after Morgan had gone. I won't think about Alys and Dan, not when Tom is missing. Let them sleep if they can, because I don't feel I shall ever sleep again.

Richard got out a jigsaw puzzle, which he spread on the kitchen table, and was soon absorbed. Ray, who had acted like a stranger

103

ever since this ghastly thing had happened, went into the hall. Bethan followed him, hungry for a crumb of comfort.

'Don't shut me out, Ray,' she implored. 'I can't bear it.'

He turned to look at her, and she saw the naked misery on his face.

'It's too much,' he said, the words harsh and laboured. 'First Trixie, now Tom. If anything happens to Tom—'

'It won't,' said Bethan sturdily. 'Tom's all right. It's just the waiting. Don't let it get to you.'

'You can't know he's all right.'

'Yes I do.'

'Are you psychic, or something?'

'Yes.' Bethan was firm. 'I'm the one who saw Linwell Johnny. Remember?'

A reluctant smile touched Ray's wide mouth, then she was in his arms, crushed against him, feeling the tautness of his misery, the ache in him for peace and comfort. She had suddenly become stronger, in charge of the situation.

'Now no more doubts,' she ordered. 'This is just one of those nasty patches that life throws at you. Next week, you'll wonder why you worried so much.'

He held her to him, drawing comfort from her warmth and certainty.

'I love you,' Bethan murmured. 'What hurts you hurts me.'

Other calls followed, from kind, caring people who were showing their concern, but every time the telephone rang it jangled the nerves of the people who were waiting for the one message they needed to hear.

Never had a day seemed so long. It felt like a hundred years since Bethan and Ray had returned to the village hall, and been confronted with the chilling picture of Tom's empty bed. Was it only this morning?

In the evening, Ray switched on the television news, not so much for information as to make a break in the awful vacuum that yawned all around them. Apathetically, they watched the usual scenes of violence and bloodshed abroad, then items of a national character. A member of the royal family had visited a hospital in the north, and a cliff erosion at a coastal resort had caused great damage.

The newscaster paused, and a picture of Southbeck appeared on the screen. Three pairs of eyes were riveted now.

'In the village of Southbeck, the search is still going on for a small boy, who disappeared during a demonstration against nuclear dumping. Demonstrators successfully averted the dumpers, but the boy, aged eight, has still not been found.'

A harsh sound from Ray drew Bethan's attention. Richard gazed fearfully at his father, as the news report continued.

105

'*Police and tracker dogs, combing the area, have made a discovery. This is the wreck of a wartime RAF plane, together with the body of an airman. The plane, and the airman's remains, have lain undisturbed in a peat-bog for over forty-five years. Although it is too soon yet for more details, a spokesman from a local airclub said that records from RAF Linwell would be consulted, in an effort to clear the mystery!*'

'How strange,' said Bethan faintly, as the weather man came on the screen to forecast rain and gales. 'How odd that only a few minutes ago, we were—'

She shivered. She had spoken to Ray from the heart about the ghost of Linwell Johnny, but in this moment she could not be sure of anything. Not long ago she had been an independent career woman. Not it was all changed, and she was in some dark, foggy world, where there were no certainties any more.

What am I doing here, she asked herself, and the answer could only be Ray. She loved him, and she was here because of him.

She stood up, and the room swam away from her. As she took a step forward, the room dissolved under her feet, and she was falling, falling.

Strong arms went round her, and Ray's voice said, 'Here now, you've had just about as much as you can take.'

Head still swirling, Bethan's vision cleared momentarily, and she had a quick snapshot of Richard's white, staring face. Poor Richard, she thought. I mustn't upset him. He's had enough.

Her eyelids drooped again, too tired to keep open, as Ray carried her upstairs. She sat on the guest-room bed as he gently pulled off her clothes, fitted her arms into one of his own pyjama jackets, which hung on her like a scarecrow. Then her head sank into the pillow, and the blessed oblivion of sleep took over.

Her last drowsy thought was, I wanted to comfort them, but they are comforting me.

When she woke, it must have been hours later, for the window was quite dark. Bethan lay for a little while, thoughts drifting through her mind. Then it all came back to her, with the shock of cold water. Tom. Where was Tom? She must get up, find out if there had been any news.

There was a dressing-gown hanging on a hook. Bethan pulled it on, and went out onto the landing, where a light had been left burning.

Nothing broke the silence. Richard must be in bed, worn out with everything that had happened. And Ray. She stood alone, crushed by the emptiness. Maybe *I'm* a ghost, she thought mournfully. Maybe all this is a dream, just a dream. No. A nightmare.

Creeping towards the stairs, so as not to

disturb the others, she paused in the dim light by the clock in the hall. Ten minutes past midnight. That's all it was. The night and its loneliness still lay ahead.

Bethan shivered, drawing the warm gown more closely around herself, but the cold came from some deep ache inside her, and nothing would ease it, or take it away.

Perhaps a warm drink would help, but it seemed too much effort even to walk downstairs into the kitchen. Pull yourself together, said a small voice in the darkness of her brain. Get a hold on yourself. What good will it do if you fall in pieces? Aren't things already bad enough?

The small needle-point of courage was still pricking. Trying to move stealthily so as to make no noise, she crept downstairs. Reaching the ground floor, her legs felt steadier. Opening the door quietly, she went into the room that looked out over the lawns to the copse of beeches beyond.

Brilliant moonlight threw long shadows onto the grass. It all looked so peaceful, as though people and their problems were of no substance. The scent of a bowl of roses, already dropping their petals, drifted through the room.

Bethan turned to cross the hall. She was almost at the kitchen door when a harsh jangling noise cut through the silence, shattering it like plate glass. A rash of shock ran over her skin in grey gooseflesh. The noise went on—and on—and on, so that she wanted to clap her hands over her ears, and shut it out. Then reality hit her like a sledgehammer. The telephone ringing, in Ray's study.

'Ray,' she gasped; then only moments later he appeared on the upstairs landing, taut and anxious, fear etched on his face. Lights went on, then he came down the stairs in a torrent of movement. He squeezed her hand briefly as he passed, then grabbed at the telephone.

Transfixed to the spot, Bethan could hear his sharp questions, the long pause whilst he listened, the taut queries, then his demand. 'Would you say that again, please? Would you say it very slowly?'

The sounds buzzed around her head like angry bees. There was another silence, punctured by Ray saying 'Yes, yes I understand.'

Oh God, thought Bethan bleakly. I can't bear it for him. If there's been an accident, then why couldn't it have been me? I don't matter. But Tom does.

The drone of voices was still going on as she raised her head, and caught sight of Richard, staring down into the hall. She stretched out her arms, willing the boy to come down to her. Hardly daring to breathe, she sensed rather than saw that something had changed.

'Well?' she croaked.

Ray let out a long sigh.

'It's all right,' he said unsteadily. 'Tom's safe. He's miles away from here, but he's safe.'

'Miles—away?'

Richard had joined them now, and was looking to the two adults, like a boy waiting for rescue from a flood.

'Let's go and sit down,' suggested Ray. 'My legs feel as though they've been knocked from under me. But Tom's safe. He's all right. Let's sit down, and I'll tell you about it.'

They sank into chairs, the elusive fragrance of the roses drifting over them like gentle rain.

'That was the police,' said Ray. 'They've had a call from a remote spot in the Scottish Highlands. Tom's there, with a couple of campers, man and woman, driving a motor-home. As far as the police can make out, this couple were driving up from the south, and stopped off at the Southbeck demonstration for a bit of a lark. They were in and out of the vehicle, all over the place, not noticing when Tom crept in and hid under some blankets. It's all a bit garbled, but I gather he was asleep when they drove off. Then when he woke up, he was too frightened to call attention to himself.'

Bethan tried to absorb all this.

'But that was—' Her mind baulked at calculation. 'But that was—ages ago.'

'Yes. Evidently the driver is one of these with an obsession for keeping on going. They didn't

110

find Tom until they were well over the border, when they were looking for somewhere to camp, in an extremely isolated area. Naturally they were thunder-struck. They started off to make a telephone call, and hit a boulder in the road, breaking a rear axle. They had to walk to the nearest place. That's why it's taken until now.'

'Tom's okay,' said Richard, summing it up for all of them. 'I think I'll go back to bed.'

'When will he be here?' asked Bethan. The last twenty-four hours had seemed a hundred years long.

'Maybe later tomorrow.'

She groped for Ray's hand.

'I'm so glad he's all right,' she whispered.

'You said he would be.' Ray gave her a weary smile. 'I think I'll go to bed too.'

Something inside her longed for the comfort of Ray's warm bulk beside her as she lay in bed. Just for solace. Just for ease. But it couldn't be now.

Bethan went upstairs.

CHAPTER ELEVEN

Sunlight filled the bedroom when Bethan awoke. She lay drowsing in relief and contentment, saying over and over again to

111

herself 'Tom's all right. Tom's coming home.'

From downstairs in the kitchen came the clatter of dishes, and the appetising aroma of breakfast floated upwards. She was just contemplating taking a shower when Ray came in with a tray. Coffee, orange-juice, toast, and one single, perfect rose, with the dew of morning still on it.

A lump came to Bethan's throat.

'You shouldn't,' she protested. 'Not when you've had so much to worry about.'

'No trouble,' he declared airily. 'Anyway, you've got Mrs. Challis to thank.'

He sat on the bed, smiling at her.

'I know it's not been easy,' he said. 'But thanks. You did help.'

He was almost the old, jaunty Ray again, but privately Bethan wondered if the events of the last two days hadn't changed them all. Ray had to go to work, he said, but he was in close contact with the police, and Tom wasn't likely to be back before evening. Mrs. Challis, the daily housekeeper, would look after Richard. They would all meet up later for Tom's return.

Kissing Bethan lightly, Ray left. She dawdled over her breakfast, glad of the chance of a few hours relief from crushing worry and strain, sorry in a way that she was leaving Richard, if only for a while.

When she had dressed, she went to say hello to Mrs. Challis, a woman of about forty, with a

112

pleasant country face. Richard sat at the kitchen table, poring over a newspaper. At a glance, Bethan saw the headline. *Small Stowaway Safe.*

With it was a picture of a hairy couple in jeans and loose T-shirts, crumpled, their arms entwined. In front of them stood Tom, grinning.

Richard's face had a closed look. It was hard to know what he was thinking. But Bethan could guess. No doubt he had been sick with worry over Tom's disappearance, as they all had. But it was the same old story. Tom was the bright, sparkling comet who lit up the sky, whilst Richard stayed in the background. In a moment of perception, Bethan knew that Tom was like his late mother, mercurial, unpredictable, demanding the eyes of those he knew. Tom had driven his mother to distraction, or so Bethan had been told. But only because they were so much alike.

She promised Richard that she would be around later, and went back to Maggie's cottage. Even after so short an absence, the four walls seemed strange. But she had things to do, and there was no time for fancy.

A telephone call to Harvey's wife produced the information that he had undergone his surgery, and would be many weeks in convalescence. Bethan also asked for the address of the absent Maggie in Australia. Whether she knew it or not, this lady had been

113

instrumental in bringing about a change in Bethan's life. A letter of thanks and explanation would be sent without delay.

There was a day to fill, so she set about sprucing up the place, both inside and out. Later she went shopping in the village, to discover that everyone knew all about Tom's escapade, and there were to be balloons and also banners saying 'Welcome Home Tom'.

There was still a lot of time before evening. Through the blur of the last nightmarish days and nights came a picture of Trash Morgan strolling across the drive at Wood Hall, unaware of their distress, intent only on sharing his personal news. Alys was back. He had brought Alys and Dan to Dyke Farm.

Up to this moment, Bethan had tucked away this piece of information in a corner of her mind. Then was not the time to deal with it. But now it must be taken out and faced.

Somehow, she had never quite rid herself of that last haunting memory: Alys weeping, choking out the words 'He doesn't love me. He doesn't love me'.

That was nearly two years ago. Before she could have second thoughts, Bethan got into her car and drove to Dyke Farm. She drew up in the yard where she had parked before, relieved to note that the fierce dog was barking this time from inside a closed barn. Again the house door stood open.

114

'Anybody there?' called Bethan, across a hall shot with sun where dust motes danced. There had been some pains to make the place look welcoming. An earthenware jug was crammed with a stiff arrangement of summer flowers.

No voice answered. From somewhere within came the murmur of conversation. Bethan moved forward, and pushed open a door. As it creaked, a small child crawling about on the carpet looked up and stared at her. Glorious red curls framed a bright little face. The boy sat back with a bump, and stuck his thumb in his mouth. Morgan put a coffee-mug down on the table, and bent to pick him up.

Alys was standing with her back to the fireplace. The same long, silky lashes over grey eyes, hair the colour of honey, only sleeker than before, neat, immaculate. There was a new quality about her. She looked more composed, more confident.

For a moment, Bethan found no words would come. Morgan saved them by saying, 'I'll go and put the kettle on.' He hoisted Dan up into his arms, and departed to the kitchen.

'Well,' said Bethan. 'Long time, no see.'

All the pent-up emotions she had struggled to contain threatened to break out and engulf her. I hope I don't cry, she thought helplessly. But part of her was still too numb for that.

'I'm glad you came,' said Alys, and that covered a lot of things. Then she lunged

115

forward, and folded her shaking sister into her arms.

'So this is it?' whispered Bethan. 'He asked you to come back, and you came.'

'Yes. Oh yes. He wants us both. He's absolutely hooked on Dan, who of course is the image of his father. We're going to stay.'

'What about the people in Vancouver?'

'They were decent about it. When they knew where I was going, they said they understood.'

'Are you happy, Alys?' asked Bethan suddenly.

'Unbelievably.'

'To tie yourself to someone as chancy and unreliable as Morgan?'

'I know it might not be easy, but I'm so happy now. And Dan belongs with Morgan. They fit like peas in a pod!'

Yes, that shows, Bethan admitted to herself. Maybe Ray was right, and children went to Morgan like lambs to a shepherd. What a strange man he was, full of talent, difficult, callous in some ways, yet with such a capability for gentleness. How could she even begin to understand him? How could Alys?

But there was a new bloom on Alys, and nothing was going to make Bethan cloud that moment.

'You're staying on here?' she asked.

'Yes. It's lovely. It's good for Dan, and to me, after Vancouver, it's like heaven.'

Morgan came back and dumped Dan on the carpet with two pan lids to clash together, went out, and returned with a tray of tea. Accepting a cup, and a shortbread biscuit, Bethan recalled that when she had last seen Morgan, it had been when he was informed at Wood Hall that Tom was missing.

'Tom's been found,' she said, marvelling that even for a few moments she had been able to let that matter recede from her mind.

Morgan smiled.

'I know. Ray telephoned. You've all had a bad time.'

It seemed such an over-simplification that Bethan didn't answer. She had this odd feeling that here in this room with these three people welded into a relationship, she had walked into a time-capsule, where no other world existed.

But there was another world out there, a world of dog-eat-dog, a rat race, a struggle for survival. What about Morgan's singing career, and his prospects, and how was he going to support Alys, who had no means of her own, and also a little red-headed baby boy?

'Are you giving up your singing career?' she asked him bluntly.

'No. Not yet. Not while there's money to be made. But I'm going to be—how shall I put it?—be more expedient; handle things better.'

You'll have to, thought Bethan with satisfaction. Because you're going to find that dealing with Mark Lime is a whole lot different from dealing with his father, who gave you too much rope, that got slacker and slacker, because although he didn't know it, he was really ill.

'Tell me about Ray,' demanded Alys, who had obviously already heard a lot from Morgan.

'Widower of thirty-four, with two sons, lives at Wood Hall, handsome—' She was going to add 'and I love him,' but stopped.

'And?' prompted Alys.

'Local hero,' concluded Bethan crisply. There were a lot of decisions still to be made.

She had stayed long enough for the first time. Making sure that Alys knew the address of Maggie's cottage, and the telephone number, Bethan drove away. Her mind was still in a whirl from so many new impressions.

Around her, people were sorting out their problems, finding solutions. But what lay ahead for Bethan? She loved Ray, and he had told her that he loved her too, but beyond that there was no clear commitment. As for her job with the Lime Agency in London, she had already hinted to Mark that her interest had weakened, and he had not made any effort to change her mind.

Back at the cottage, she telephoned Ray, and discovered that Tom would arrive back in Southbeck at seven o'clock in the evening. Members of the boys' village band had been called together, to play something jaunty if not very tuneful, and no doubt there would be a small crowd.

Bethan arranged to meet Ray and Richard there. When she arrived, sure enough people were milling about awaiting the police car, and photographers from local newspapers hovered.

There was a heady buzz of excitement running round, and Bethan reflected that for a small village, Southbeck had known a good deal of drama during the last few days.

Over on the edge of the crowd, Ray leaned against his car, Richard standing uneasily by him. The boy doesn't like this much, she thought. All this fuss only worries and embarrasses him. She went over to join them.

Ray greeted her cheerily, but no more so than any friend. He wouldn't make a fuss in public. He was not that kind of man. But she felt forlornly that it was a long time now since they had been alone together.

Seven o'clock came and went, with the boys' band turning up, dropping their music, arguing amiably. A police car appeared along the road. The bandmaster raised his baton, and the players struck up with a march.

The car stopped. One officer got out, and opened the door. A policewoman stepped down, then Tom. His fair hair stuck up around his head, his smooth cheeks were flushed, his eyes searched around for his family. Spotting

119

Ray, he gave a yelp like a Red Indian, and dived towards him.

The band went into 'For He's a Jolly Good Fellow', a ragged cheer ran round, and cameras flashed.

People surged around as Ray exchanged remarks with the police officers. Tom got in his father's car, but leaned out of the window, grinning hugely. Perhaps I should let them go home to Wood Hall and have this time alone, thought Bethan vaguely. She was disorientated, exhausted with so many events, and so many worries.

'You're coming, aren't you?'

Richard was tugging at her sleeve. She looked down at his face, anxious and entreating.

'Well—'

Ray was still talking to the police officer, and there was no help from that direction.

'Yes, come. Please come. I want you to come.'

Wordlessly she got in the back of the car with Richard. Five minutes later, Ray slumped in the driving-seat. He sagged back for a moment, as though under an enormous weight. Then he straightened, started the car, and moved off.

No doubt father and newly-returned son would have to do some talking, and already Bethan was wondering if it wouldn't have been better to leave them to it. But Richard's silent appeal still reached out to her.

At Wood Hall, she went to the kitchen to cut sandwiches, leaving Ray, Richard and Tom alone for a vital few minutes. When she ventured to join them, Tom had the look about him of a boy who had been severely reprimanded. But it wouldn't last, Bethan knew. Tom would bubble through it, ready for the next adventure.

'They go take a bath,' said Ray sternly. 'Then they can eat. Then they go to bed.'

Quiet descended. For the first time, Bethan and Ray were alone together.

'I'm absolutely bushed,' he confessed, his voice hoarse. 'What all this has been like for you, I can't imagine. Do you think you can put up with us?'

It was a misleadingly simple question, but Bethan didn't intend to go looking for complications.

'Yes,' she said firmly.

'But you're used to the glamour and the glitz. Won't you miss all that?'

'Maybe, a little.' She smiled. 'But I'll be gaining a lot more.'

He held her in his arms, drawing help and comfort from her. Although they both needed rest, they talked for a long time. Bethan couldn't go back to the cottage unless Ray took her by car, and he would not leave the boys alone in the house.

In the guest-room, she reflected that if the

villagers knew she was at Wood Hall, and most of them did, very few would believe that she and Ray slept in different rooms. She lay drowsing in the darkness. Another time, another place, she told herself.

Sleep came as a friend.

CHAPTER TWELVE

But she awoke far too soon, all sorts of questions clamouring in her head. It was as though, now Tom was safely restored to his family, a waterfall of other uncertainties could be undammed. She had spent time in Southbeck, immersed in Ray, drawn into local problems because of him. He loved her; he had said so. He had also said, 'Can you put up with us?'

What he had not made clear was how he saw their future together. How could Bethan sort her own affairs out if she did not know what Ray had in mind?

So far, he had not mentioned marriage, and even in this day and age Bethan could not conceive of him settling for a more free and easy arrangement. Nor, if she was honest, would she have wanted that for herself. She was at a point in her life when she was ready for commitment.

Reviewing her own actions, she began to

wonder if she hadn't been a bit hasty, running out of a glittering job in London, when the future was by no means certain. She still worked for the Lime Agency, although in these last few weeks she had been casual in her approach.

Suppose Ray only wanted a weekend girlfriend? If Bethan lost her job at the agency, she couldn't live on fresh air, nor could she keep on camping out in someone else's cottage.

She tossed and shuffled in the bed, wondering where that glorious, carefree happiness had gone. Perhaps she had been a fool. An eligible man like Ray Allington could never have been short of likely partners. Maybe she had assumed too much.

I'm no better than Alys, she thought ruefully. Alys was dazzled, had her head turned, mesmerised by a dream. Surely Bethan, older, more sophisticated, should have been more aware.

Uncomfortable feelings persisted, although she told herself that these doubts were due to reaction, the strain of the last few days. By the time she had showered and dressed, Mrs. Challis was already in the kitchen, and the homely smell of breakfast wafted on the air.

They don't need me, Bethan told herself, watching the boys tucking in to eggs, toast and marmalade. Ray had already spoken of his backlog of work that had mounted up recently.

He was preoccupied, and that was understandable. Richard, as always, said little. Tom was full of chatter, as the boys were due to go away to holiday-camp on Saturday for a week, and his mind was leaping away to that.

Bethan glanced at Ray.

'Give me a lift back to the village when you go.'

'You're going to the cottage?'

'Yes. Then back to London. It's time I came down to earth.'

There was a small sound of dismay from Richard, scarcely audible over the sound of Tom crunching toast. Ray stood up. Bethan squeezed Richard's shoulder, then Tom's, and left.

Ray didn't say much on the drive to Southbeck, but outside the cottage he leaned over and kissed her, then drew away, smiling ruefully.

'What we've been through so far has been pretty hectic, but we have all the time in the world.'

For once Bethan was silent, and if he suspected that she had any doubts, he gave no sign. As she unlocked the cottage door, she could hear the telephone ringing.

Picking up the receiver, Bethan at once recognised the irate voice of Mark Lime.

'At last,' he said tartly. 'You're worse than a needle in a haystack. Do I take it you still work for this firm?'

'Sorry,' she murmured, professional politeness surfacing. 'It's been all systems go, and—'

'So what do you think it's been like here? You either work here, or you don't.'

'Will do,' agreed Bethan, reflecting how some solutions presented themselves. It took her half an hour to clear up things at the cottage, fill up the car with petrol, and start for London.

Nearer the city, the traffic was horrendous, and she needed all her concentration, although Mark Lime's angry words still rang in her head. During her years with Harvey, he had never raised his voice to her. She drove to her own flat, changed into a smart outfit, applied careful make-up, and checked in at the office.

The place was seething with activity. A new girl with a startling haircut sat at a computer, and the main desk was awash with mail. From the telephone, putting his hand over the mouthpiece, Mark Lime said, 'First of all, we'll sort out the paperwork; then there are clients to meet, people to entertain.'

By the time Bethan crawled back to her flat it was nearly midnight. Southbeck seemed as distant as a dream, a place she had read about sometime, but almost forgotten. Next day she found time to ask Mark about Harvey.

'He's okay,' he replied dismissively. 'He'll be a long time recovering, so don't think things are going to be the same.'

For the next few days Mark worked her hard, no doubt to establish the relationship. In a way Bethan welcomed it, for it precluded the necessity to think about anything else.

As the weekend approached, her mind refused a decision. Should she trot along to Southbeck again, like some obedient puppy, or await events? Latish on Thursday night, her telephone rang. Familiar joy flooded through her at Ray's voice. She loved him. He was the man who made her life whole and meaningful.

'Are you ready for Saturday?' he asked her, a teasing note in his voice.

'Saturday?'

'I'm arranging a party here. I thought it might be a good idea to announce our engagement—that is, if you are willing.'

There was a pause. Then Bethan said, 'Do I take it you are asking me to marry you?'

'I am. Pretty soon. I don't see what either of us has to wait for.'

'You take my breath away,' she said in a low voice. In the short space of minutes, everything had changed.

'The answer is yes,' she said, suddenly overwhelmed by the idea of a husband, two step-sons, a country house, and a whole new social set-up.

On Saturday Ray arranged to pick Bethan up during the afternoon, so that they could spend some time together before the party in the evening. A cold buffet meal was to be prepared and served by Mrs. Challis, and with the boys away at summer camp, it was a strictly adult affair.

At Wood Hall, Ray put his arm round Bethan as they strolled in the garden. He paused in the most beautiful spot, with a vista of rolling fields, and the scent of roses all around.

'I couldn't put into words how much this place means to me,' he confided. 'Trixie loathed it. All she wanted was to get away. But you and me—we have something we can build on, we can share. And I love you. You came into my life when I most needed you.'

He brought a small leather box out of his pocket. Inside, cushioned on ruby velvet, was a flawless circlet of diamonds that must have been worth a small fortune.

Bethan, accustomed as she was to the opulent jewellery of London society, gasped.

Ray slipped it on her finger.

'It's right for you,' he said with satisfaction. 'It's been in the Allington family for years. Trixie liked junk jewellery; clanking beads and gypsy hoops. She wouldn't look at a thing like this. But on you, it's right.'

And it was, except that perhaps it was a little on the large side, and slipped on Bethan's slender finger. Suddenly her eyes were full of tears, not only for the ring, but for all it signified: hope, trust, and promise. She turned to Ray, and buried her face in his shoulder. There was so much to say, but words choked her.

'I'm happy,' she whispered. 'Truly happy, for the first time in as long as I can remember.'

In a daze of contentment streaked with resolution, Bethan went to prepare for the evening's celebrations. In the chancy world of show business, she had seen so many relationships totter and crumble, that she was determined to bring to her own marriage those qualities that would give life a richer and more enduring quality.

By eight o'clock, people were arriving: various locals, wellknown to Ray, but so far only names to Bethan; a crowd from the Linwell Air Club, headed by Captain Percy Harris, who had the sort of twinkle in his eye that said 'I told you so'; Julie, of the shaggy mane, who flashed Bethan a sunny smile.

Then Alys and Trash Morgan, looking at ease in each other's company. Little Dan must have been left in charge of the elderly housekeeper.

Glancing at Alys and Morgan together, Bethan reflected ruefully that if it hadn't been for Morgan, she would never have met Ray in the first place. Life was odd in some ways.

Whatever differences Morgan and Alys might have had in the past, they seemed to have resolved them now. Bethan was content to let it go at that.

Speech-making was at a minimum, as everyone seemed to know why they were here. After drinks and a toast, talk turned to the mystery at the air base, where the remains of an unknown bomber pilot had lain undisturbed and unidentified for more than forty years. Inevitably Bethan's thoughts turned to one of the first conversations she had ever had with Ray, when he had taken her into his study and shown her souvenirs of Second World War pilots.

It had put her so poignantly in mind of her father's older brother, David Blake, a wartime flyer whose disappearance had never been accounted for. Although the likelihood of there being any connection between the recent discovery at Linwell and Bethan's family mystery seemed remote, a note of melancholy chimed in the corridors of her mind.

She was back to the evening when she had been at odds with Ray, disturbed and upset by their misunderstanding, wandering around a derelict aircamp in the gathering dark.

Then, from out of nowhere, he had appeared, a man with dark, haunted eyes, dressed in bloodstained flying-gear, pleading to be shown the way home. He had been desperate, imploring. And it was to Bethan he had spoken. 'I've got to get back to base,' he had gasped.

'Where is it?'

'You've seen Linwell Johnny,' Ray had said afterwards, half joking, half serious.

How could Bethan not feel highly involved, seeing Linwell Johnny? It was to her he had appeared. 'I've got to get back to base,' he had gasped. 'I've *got* to get back to base.'

Listening to talk, she discovered that Linwell Air Club was to come to a complete standstill on Monday, whilst the remains of the unknown bomber pilot were transported with full military honours to a local RAF cemetery. The oak coffin was to bear a plaque with the words 'unknown airman' inscribed upon it.

Records had been scoured, and every plane that had crashed near Linwell had been accounted for. But it was hoped that this funeral would lay to rest the ghost that had haunted Linwell so long.

Hearing all these plans, Bethan knew that she must attend this simple ceremony. If she didn't, there would for ever be left a blank area in her mind that nothing would fill. An appeal unanswered. It meant taking extra time off from the agency, but at least now she had a clearer idea of the future, and that her days there were numbered anyway.

The story of the Southbeck anti-dumping demonstration seemed to have died almost overnight, and a particularly vociferous group of MPs devoted to country conservation were now hotly defending the rights of local citizens. For the time being, the threat of dumping had been lifted.

By midnight, the party was breaking up, Ray standing, his arm around Bethan, as they drove away into the night. Nothing is going to separate us now, she promised herself. They were committed.

No words were needed, for each understood. The house had quietened. All that lingered was the echo of laughter, and the chink of wineglasses.

Gently Ray took Bethan's hand, and led her upstairs to his room, where she had not been before. Subdued light showed comfortable, if somewhat subdued furnishings. There was a kingsized bed, but some sixth sense told Bethan that Ray had never shared it with Trixie. That when Trixie went, a lot of changes had been made.

Ray opened the door of an en-suite bathroom, turned on taps, and laid out sumptuous fluffy towels. Without a word, Bethan went to him.

His fingers, urgent and trembling, pulled at the fastenings of her dress. Soft garments fell to the floor, as she stood in rosy nakedness, her body throbbing with the delight that was to come. Slipping off his clothes, Ray's mouth hungrily sought her breasts, her nipples that hardened in his mouth.

'I can't wait,' she gasped.

'Yes you can,' he muttered hoarsely, lifting her into the warm, scented water, and laving water over her limbs in a way that made her shudder with delight.

Moments later, she was wrapped in a warm towel, his hands bringing messages of desire that made the blood run under her skin like fire.

He carried Bethan to the bed, where she lay half-dazed and dreaming. A moment later, his own naked flesh pressed against her. She turned towards him as a flower turns to the sun, urgent for warmth and nourishment and beauty. His hands were strong and gentle, but their readiness for each other was so great that as he entered her with such ease and delight, a great tremor ran through her.

For a moment they lay, irrevocably bonded. There was no hurry, only the supreme joy of union. Then—then—the star-shot blackness of climax.

Cradled in Ray's arms, Bethan slept like a baby.

CHAPTER THIRTEEN

On Sunday afternoon, Bethan telephoned Mary Lime to find out how Harvey was progressing.

His convalescence was slow, but he was cheerful, and seemed to have come to terms with the change in his circumstances.

Then Bethan asked for Mark's home telephone number. She owed him an explanation, and within the next few days she would sort out her responsibilities to the agency, a place which she would now leave, and then act accordingly.

Mark was non-committal on the telephone when she spoke of the airman's funeral, and he clearly regarded it as one of her hare-brained ideas. She promised to be back at the agency as soon as possible, and hung up before he could go into detail. She and Ray had the rest of the day to spend together, and there was not a minute of it that she wished to lose.

It was glorious summer, fine, warm, and he drove her in his car around all the areas his business controlled: long, endless fields where flowers and bulbs were produced; smart garden centres, bright with visitors, arrays of plants, sunny posters beaming down from the walls. It was a little overwhelming, but Bethan could see how his heart was here, and how much of himself he had given to create such an enterprise.

In the evening, they found a friendly pub, and bought a simple meal. The day had slipped through Bethan's fingers.

Monday was different. In the morning, Ray

133

left for business, returning for the afternoon ceremony when the remains of the unknown wartime bomber crew member were to be laid to rest. Ray looked sombre in a dark suit, and Bethan shivered at the memory of her ghostly apparition.

She sat silently beside Ray in the car, and by the time they reached the RAF war-grave cemetery, rain was sweeping across the empty grey landscape. As well as uniformed men in impeccable formation, a crowd of damp and dismal onlookers stood around. A chaplain read solemn words and pronounced a benediction. But it was the bugler playing the solemn notes of the 'Last Post' that brought tears flooding to Bethan's eyes.

Soil and pebbles rattled down on the oak coffin. It was over. Surely there would be some peace now, some end to a tragic story. Bethan began to feel a little better. Ahead lay a promising future. Sadness could be put aside.

Ray drove her to Southbeck, where she lingered for a brief snack before driving back to London. Soon these journeys would cease. But at the present there were obligations to fulfil, details to settle.

She left reluctantly, settling down to the drive. This was a quiet time of day, and traffic was sparse. Scarcely six miles out of Southbeck, long, waving grass edged the roadway, with fields, blurred by rain, shimmering away on either side.

Bethan wound down the window for air. Gazing ahead, her blue eyes suddenly sharpened. On her side of the road, heading in the direction she had just left, a small, solitary figure had come into view. Walking awkwardly through the rough, wet grass; lifting up feet and putting them down with a sort of plodding determination. Too small for a tramp or hitch-hiker. Some local lad who had missed his lift home from school?

She reduced speed to cruising, for there was no other traffic to bother her. As she drove nearer, a gasp rose in her throat, for the boy, whose eyes had been fixed frowningly on the uneven ground, looked up, recognised her, and his face broadened into a smile of relief. Richard Allington. Dark-haired, serious Richard, who supposedly was safely away at summer camp for the rest of the week.

Richard flung his junior size rucksack down on the grass. Bethan braked gently, and got out of the car.

'What's this?' she asked, hiding her puzzlement under a show of cheerfulness. 'How come I find you on a lonely road, on your own, when you should be safely at camp?'

'I left,' said Richard simply.

'But—' Bethan searched for the right words. 'What happened? Did you get into trouble? Were you ill?'

135

There were all sorts of other questions besides those.

'No. There were just some things I wanted to ask you about. I wanted to see you, see you as soon as I could.'

'But you would have seen me when you came home.'

'That's *a week*.'

No doubt to a young boy a week seemed an endless period of time.

'But how did you get here? Didn't anybody know you'd gone?'

'I made sure they didn't,' replied Richard simply. 'I got the train to Marfield Junction, but that's near as it goes. Anyway—I found you.'

He was congratulating himself on the turn of events, but Bethan felt nothing but dismay. She had been in the act of leaving Southbeck, at least until Saturday. Now she would have to sort this out.

It seemed hard on the boy that he managed to walk into her line of vision just as she was leaving. But with the innocence of childhood, he had assumed that when at last he arrived at Wood Hall, Bethan would be there.

Disappointment for his mistake filled her. Ray was working, Mrs. Challis wasn't expecting to care for the boys this week, and Bethan was on her way.

She stepped forward and gave him a brief

hug. His stiff shoulders worried her. Richard wasn't the one who ran away. It had always been Tom, and with him it was a game.

'Come on, get in the car,' she said kindly. 'We'll sort something out.'

The solution in this case was to drive back to Wood Hall, telephone Ray, and see what he suggested.

'Didn't you like the camp?' she asked, striving very hard to keep a light note between them.

'It was all right.'

'What about Tom?'

'Tom's all right.'

Silence fell, like a damp, foggy blanket. Because he was acutely sensitive to atmosphere, perhaps Richard had picked up vibrations that did not reassure him. He seemed to have shrunk inside himself. Although he had been glad to see Bethan, he didn't need anyone to tell him that already his plan had gone wrong.

To her relief, Ray's car was parked on the drive at Wood Hall. As she and Richard approached, Ray came out, a sheaf of papers in his hand. His face registered first surprise, then incredulity.

'Look who came,' she called out, hoping this wasn't going to be too difficult. It was Richard she was worried about. The minor inconvenience to herself didn't matter. All she wished for was that Richard wouldn't be too hurt in any way.

'So what's this?' Not unkindly, nevertheless Ray seemed to speak abruptly.

Richard's mouth clamped in an obstinate line. He could see there wasn't going to be the way out he had imagined.

'He—he left the camp,' Bethan said. 'He wanted to talk to—to someone. So he got the train to Marfield Junction, then started walking to Southbeck. Wasn't it lucky that I was driving by just then?'

She beamed at Ray, looking for support, and, give him his due, he sent her a rueful smile, as if to imply that he knew she was aiming to keep down the tension.

'Better come inside,' he said.

They went to the beautiful room overlooking the garden, Richard standing awkwardly on the rich carpet, more like a boy caught breaking in than a child of the house.

'So what happened?' asked Ray, the natural warmth of fatherhood stealing through. 'Don't you know this worries us? Was it so bad? I thought you were going to manage quite well. If I'd thought you would run away—'

'Tom's always running away,' burst out Richard. 'But that's not why. I wanted to talk to Bethan.' The name dropped quite naturally from his lips. 'Now I can't, because she won't be here.'

'What about?' asked Ray.

'It's private.' He had stiffened up again.

'I'll stay,' said Bethan swiftly.

'No.' This was Richard, who could pick up a mood or atmosphere like a sparrow picking up crumbs.

'Well, he's got to go back,' said Ray firmly. 'They'll be frantic there when they find he's gone. He's their responsibility. Besides—'

Bethan knew what he was going to say—that you didn't walk out on things on impulse, however strong the urge might be.

Richard sent an imploring glance to her.

'He's right, Richard,' she told him quietly. 'It's only a few more days after all. I'll be here on Saturday, and we can talk as long as you like.'

The boy wasn't happy with the situation, but he saw that he would have to accept it.

'Do you promise?' His dark eyes stared piercingly at Bethan.

'I promise,' she said.

The rest was anticlimax, Ray making a telephone call and Bethan setting out once again for London. She hadn't let Richard down, she told herself, nor had she failed to support Ray. What had been brought home to her were the dark rivers and currents of family life. It was a new role, maybe disturbing, but no doubt with compensating joys.

In any case, she had accepted it unreservedly, and remembering the promises she had made to herself about her marriage to Ray, she had no intention of not facing up to any situation.

It was too late today for any contact with the Lime Agency, but Tuesday morning, bright and early, Bethan turned up before Mark Lime appeared. Am I going to miss all this, she wondered? She scarcely thought so. There would be plenty to occupy her with a new life in Southbeck, and inexorably, she had already been drawn into the web of the family.

It was not an unwelcome feeling. For so long, Bethan had been alone. Those days were rapidly becoming part of the past.

Mark Lime greeted her in a perfunctory fashion, and immediately sketched out a list of what he expected of her this week. When she found a spare moment, Bethan searched out the copy of her employment contract, checked that one month's notice was required, and spent her lunch-hour composing the necessary letter.

She spent one evening on a visit to Harvey and Mary Lime. The old affection between Harvey and Bethan was there. She could feel it, could almost have touched it, but his major illness had knocked a good deal of the pep out of him. Harvey seemed happy to chuckle over Bethan's account of all the goings-on in Southbeck. She would miss him, and he would miss her, but life was like that.

Friday came at last. Bethan couldn't wait to throw a few things into a suitcase and leave for

Southbeck. Looking round what was really a very pleasant flat, she now wondered how she had managed to stick it for so long. The sooner she got the place wound up, the better.

It was very late when she reached Southbeck, too late to see Ray, so she passed a peaceful night at the cottage, and telephoned him in the morning. He expected to be back at Wood Hall with both boys at midday. They would all be together then.

Mrs. Challis had left a meal ready for them. Tom bubbled over with all the things he had to tell about the week at camp. He had struck up a friendship with another boy from a neighbouring village, where horses and ponies were bred, and raced and stabled, and so was anxious to accept an invitation to visit over there, provided his father would co-operate.

Richard said nothing, but Bethan knew he was relieved that Tom would be out of the way. Also, maybe his father, she wouldn't wonder. Richard was a boy who would seldom open up his heart to anyone at all. Especially someone from whom he feared a rebuke, or criticism.

Ray drove off with Tom. Softly, softly, Bethan told herself. Richard, without meeting her eye, said, 'I see you're wearing the ring.'

Young boys didn't usually pay much attention to things like that, and Bethan was surprised.

'Your father gave it to me,' she explained. 'It

141

means we're going to be married.'

'That ring means a lot to him. So you must mean a lot to him, or he wouldn't give it to you.'

'Why did you come home on Monday?' asked Bethan. She didn't say run away. It had too many interpretations.

'There was this story in the newspapers, on the radio, and the camp leader had a portable TV. It was on that too. About this airman who had just been found near Linwell. Nobody knew who he was. Nobody cared.'

'Yes they did,' said Bethan, a shade sharply. 'A lot of people cared. He was given a full military funeral, and now he can rest in peace.'

'But it's so sad.' One glistening tear rolled down Richard's face. 'I couldn't bear it. Dad wouldn't care. Tom would think I was off my head. But I knew you'd understand. I just wanted to talk to you.'

Bless the child, he was so sensitive; it was like being born with one skin short.

'You mustn't fret,' said Bethan gently. 'It all goes back a long way. And it's not really part of our lives.'

'Yes it is.' Richard's chin had a stubborn line. 'If Tom hadn't run away, people would never have been searching there. It was through Tom, although he doesn't care tuppence.'

'Can't we forget it?' asked Bethan.

'I want you to take me to see the place where

142

he's buried,' said Richard. 'Then to the place where the plane was found.'

Bethan frowned.

'Oh, I don't think—'

'Please. Now. Before the others come back.'

Richard stood up, determination in every line of him.

CHAPTER FOURTEEN

He emanated so much tension that Bethan warned herself to weigh her words. If she had wondered at all about why he wanted to confide in her, this was one thing she had not considered. But now she could see that such a story would move Richard, when it would leave most people uninvolved. For it concerned a loner, a one-off, and Richard had empathy for such things as this.

'Right,' said Bethan briskly. 'Going to the RAF burial-ground is no trouble. We can drive there. But the site of the crashed plane is something different. We'll have to do a lot of muddy walking. Go and find your wellington boots, whilst I write a note telling your father we're popping out.'

As he hurried away, it was almost as if she had lifted a weight from him. If she had refused, perhaps it would have rankled with

Richard in future days. Today, she supposed, would do as well as any.

At the cemetery, he stood in awkward silence. The rough soil covering the new grave was glutinous with rain. It would be weeks yet before the plot was tidied and marked. All around were the simple identical crosses of other graves. Some had a few flowers. Most had not.

'He's with his friends,' said Richard simply. It seemed to comfort him a little.

'For heaven's sake, let's get out of here,' Bethan said.

When they were in the car, she sat pondering how best to approach the site of the recently discovered crashed plane. No road led to it, no lane or farm track. The general consensus of opinion seemed to be that in emergency, the pilot had been trying to make Linfield aerodrome in a damaged machine, and had crashed a couple of miles short of his destination.

Fond though she had become of this countryside, Bethan doubted that her bump of direction was good enough to take her exactly to the spot, without wasting time and energy.

'We'll drive to the Air Club,' she announced. 'Somebody there will know more about it than I do.'

She was disappointed to find no evidence of Captain Harris being around, but the duty officer for the day listened to her with an unsmiling face, tapping his pen against a note-pad as she asked for directions.

'I'm not so sure this is a good idea, Miss—?'

'Blake.'

'Miss Blake. We don't want the general public tramping all over the plane, and in any case, what is there to see? Just a lot of excavations, and shattered junk.'

'Yes,' she agreed quietly. Perhaps it was a foolish idea, and maybe she hadn't been firm enough with Richard.

'Look,' she said, 'I have a boy waiting out there. I think this is one of those cases of hero-worship. He's a quiet, serious boy. We won't cause any trouble.'

'Then it's your responsibility entirely. I'll tell you how to get there, but I'd like you to promise me that you aren't going to encourage hordes of other kids to swarm all over the place.'

'Not a chance.'

He took her to the window, and gave her brief directions. He was back to his papers before Bethan closed the door.

Richard was already out of the car, so she locked up, and set off in the general direction that the duty officer had indicated.

The ground was slippery and squelchy under their feet. The Air Base buildings receded, just fields, unfenced, wide as prairies, stretching

145

away all around.

'When you come to the dyke, follow that,' the duty officer had advised. 'Then there's a tree that was struck by lightning. You'll need to branch off left, but if there's a crop in the field, I'm afraid you'll have to go all the way round.'

There was a crop of wheat in the field, and by the time they reached the vicinity of the excavations, Bethan's feet, unaccustomed to country walking, were tingling.

Richard was like a dog straining at the leash. He pounded on ahead of her, cheeks ruddy in the fresh air, an alertness and urgency about him Bethan had not seen before.

'Richard, be careful,' she called, seeing the great piles of peat-black earth that had been dug away to reveal what remained of the crashed plane. The site was a quagmire of mud and desolation, the stark remains of the bomber-plane looking like some pathetic skeleton.

An attempt had been made to rope off the area, with rope whose bits of red plastic fluttered forlornly in the wind. As the duty officer had said, there really wasn't anything to see, except deep holes gouged out of the earth, and the piles of soil they had dislodged.

Bethan glanced at her watch. It would take them at least an hour to return to Wood Hall, and she didn't want to keep Ray hanging about, wondering where on earth they had got to.

Richard was prowling around the perimeter, eyes on the great hunks of metal that had formerly been among the lords of the air. One of the propellers was bent into weird shapes, and another was missing entirely. The wings were shattered, and the nose of the plane broken off like a gigantic aluminium eggshell.

The pathetic cockpit, with its sodden safety-straps, brought a tightness to Bethan's throat.

'Time to go,' she said.

'Just five minutes. I want to take a souvenir back for Dad.'

What on earth was the boy after? There was nothing here but twisted metal and craters of mud. Then light dawned. Richard was after something to please his father, something to add to his collection of memorabilia.

Before she could stop him, he was scrambling down the side of a slope where earth had been gouged out, at the bottom of which lay all sorts of shattered bits of the broken aircraft. He started off on his feet, but the slope consisted of shifting, treacherous soil, so that almost at once, he was slithering on his bottom.

Alarmed now, she moved to the place, standing well back where she could see him. He was yards below her, as he sorted for a hand-sized piece of metal. She didn't like it, she didn't like it a bit, and this time he must do as he was told.

'Climb out, because I'm leaving,' she said.

He recognised that he had run out of time and forbearance.

'Right. Stand back.'

He hurled his trophy so that it fell on the grass beside her. Then he started his climb. His first three steps were no problem, then his weight caused the loose soil to start shifting. It slithered down in a most sinister fashion, gaining momentum each time Richard tried again.

Oh God, moaned Bethan inside her head, please let him get out. But fear was gnawing at her.

Richard was on all fours now. Panting, he raised his head and grinned. He doesn't see the danger, she told herself dumbly. He was only a child, and even a sensitive child's horizons were limited.

Within a short way from the top, he stopped, straining for breath.

'Dad ought to be pleased,' was all he said.

He should get out now, she told herself, a trickle of relief in her veins. Impulsively, she leaned forward, and reached for his muddy hand. His grasp was surprisingly strong, but when he was only one step from the top, he pulled his hand free, maybe to retain his masculine pride.

He was still delighted with himself when he stood on the grass beside her. Picking up his trophy, Richard gave her a beaming smile.

'You were worried, weren't you?'

'Yes. I see no sense in being foolhardy.'

'But if I couldn't have scrambled up there, I'd have tried another place.'

'Supposing the earth all caved in on top of you?'

'But it didn't, did it?'

They started on the journey back. Bethan had never seen Richard looking so dishevelled. His clothes were stained with mud, his face and hands streaked with dirt. Bethan was silent, but the incident seemed to have loosened Richard's tongue. He chatted about boys at school, and the things they collected, coming back each time to the collection in his father's study.

Without knowing it, he was revealing to Bethan some of the things that had made him so introspective. Tom had been his mother's favourite. Richard, whose qualities were of the quieter kind, was desperately trying to win his father's approval.

Back at Linwell Air Base, Bethan gazed doubtfully at the boy's jeans, which were soaked through with mud. She spread a rug on the seat of her clean, unblemished car, telling him to sit on that. As she did so, she noticed that the duty officer had seen their arrival, as he stood by a window.

Ray's car was back at Wood Hall. Before Bethan parked, Richard said to her, 'Don't say anything to Dad about what I've got, I want to clean it up first.'

Bethan felt grubby, and Richard would need a wash and change. She called out 'Hello there,' and went straight up to her room. Richard hared up the stairs with his precious prize.

When she came down again in a clean shirt and jeans, Ray was waiting for her. He looked calm and relaxed.

'Well? Where have you been? Or aren't I allowed to know?'

'Er—' It wasn't a secret, but Bethan didn't want to give Richard away. She decided on a compromise.

'He told me he was interested in the airman they found in the old wartime plane. He wanted to see the place where he was buried.'

'That was very understanding of you.'

It was not the answer she had expected, and her heart lifted, finding again some new facet of Ray's character that brought her joy. Wordlessly, she went into his arms, and they stood, locked together, until the sound of Richard's door opening made them break apart.

The boy still had the look of someone entrusted with an important mission, although he hadn't decided that the time for handing over his surprise was just yet. He glanced at his father.

'Are you two going out?'

'I don't think so,' Ray replied. 'Not just now.

Although I have to pick up Tom at the stables before long.'

Ray glanced at his son, obviously puzzled by the mysterious something that was motivating Richard.

'Do you want to go out?' he asked.

'*No thank you.* I've only just got home.'

Bethan and Ray went outside to sit on the white-painted seat that commanded a glorious view of the garden.

'Shall I take you out for a celebration dinner?' asked Ray, his arm around her. 'Just the two of us. I could get Mrs. Challis to baby-sit.'

Wherever they were, Bethan was happy, so long as they were together.

'Let me take you out,' Ray coaxed. 'I want to show off my beautiful wife-to-be. And wear your ring.'

His last words were like an icicle penetrating the warmth and love with which she had been glowing. Since returning from the site of the crashed bomber plane, she had showered and changed, then hurried downstairs to be with Ray. She didn't glance at her left hand, but she knew the ring was not there.

Perhaps I left it upstairs, said a small voice of hope not entirely extinguished. But she knew she hadn't, although at the first chance she would go and check.

It came quite soon. Richard appeared,

reporting that the telephone was ringing. Bethan and Ray went indoors, whilst Richard returned to his own pursuits.

A minute later Bethan went upstairs, the weight of doubt heavy inside her. She checked the shower, the wash-bowl, the dressing-table, her own personal luggage, and every other place she could think of. The box for the ring lay innocently in a drawer, but it was empty. Dismayed, she sat down on the bed.

Think, she told herself. Think calmly and clearly.

She let her mind go back to her arrival at Wood Hall, when she knew she had been wearing the ring. She had been aware of it as sunshine had glittered on the stones whilst her hands controlled the steering-wheel of the car. At Wood Hall also, she knew she hadn't removed it. And she had noticed the duty officer glancing at it when she had asked him for directions.

A picture flashed into her head, of Richard grasping both her hands as he hauled himself up through the mud. That was what had happened. The ring was loose, and had slipped off. In the urgency of her fear, Bethan had failed to notice.

She wasn't going to tell Ray, because he didn't know anything about their trip to the excavated site. And even if he did, she wouldn't have told him.

What Bethan must do was go back and recover it, even though the place depressed her, and she had no desire to see it again. But Richard had been nearly at the top; the ring must have fallen there, and maybe she could just reach down and recover it, without too much trouble. One thing was certain. She couldn't face telling Ray that she had lost it.

How to get away without either Ray or Richard suspecting? She went in search of Richard, who was still busy polishing up his trophy.

'Richard, I've got to go out. I want to take my car into a service-station and get the tyres pumped up.'

'Want me to come with you?'

'No, you'd only be bored. Why don't you go with your father to the stables? You might find that more interesting.'

Richard looked as though he doubted it, but he was in a good mood and offered no objection. She spun the same tale to Ray, who smiled at her good-humouredly.

'I could do that for you.'

'No. I can manage. Honestly.'

He gave her a friendly hug, and half an hour later the Allingtons had gone and Bethan was on her way to Linwell.

Please let me find it, she prayed. Please. *Please.*

Somehow, the story of the unknown airman

had taken too much hold on their lives.

The same duty officer was around.

'I lost my ring at the excavation site,' Bethan said.

She didn't give him chance to comment, but set off walking.

CHAPTER FIFTEEN

Her feet were already sore and tender before she started, but it was no use thinking about that. Without Richard trotting enthusiastically along behind her it seemed even more tedious than before. This time the loneliness of the place was really getting to her. Once the Air Base had been left behind, there was no one around for miles.

A light plane droned overhead, lifting Bethan's spirits a little, as she remembered the hour she had spent with Captain Harris, and the bright, unlimited blue of the morning. Flying still fascinated her; there was this lift of the spirit, this urge to soar away from the earth and its bonds.

Maybe a drop of David Blake's blood still lurked in her veins. He had been a wartime pilot, and the stories of his adventures had coloured her childhood.

But her interest was nowhere near an

obsession, and she would talk the matter over with Ray. She wanted their relationship to be as perfect as it could be, because she was beginning, stumblingly, to know what love was. That love wanted the best for those you cared for, even if it meant giving up something yourself.

A sixth sense told Bethan that Ray would not ask her to give up the idea of learning to fly, that he would not be so dominating. Whatever happened, they would sort it out together.

Apart from the nagging worry about the ring, she felt more cheerful. It must be there, she told herself. Maybe I can lie on the grass, reach down and pick it up. She didn't dare to think what might happen if she couldn't find it. The ring meant a great deal to Ray. He himself had said so, and Richard had echoed the same thought.

It seemed a lot further to the tree struck by lightning, and she knew herself to be tired, although being faint-hearted would bring her nothing. Bethan skirted the field of wheat, as she had done with Richard. Not much further now.

She refused to let herself think of the consequences if she couldn't see the ring within easy seconds of reaching the site. But she couldn't quell an unpleasant memory of how the soil had slithered and shifted. If that had happened, she could never find the ring, and neither could anyone else.

Reaching the site, Bethan's eyes roamed anxiously over the fluttering red pennants, the trampled grass all around, the mountains of dislodged earth. It all looked exactly the same as when she and Richard had left. Hopefully, she could spot what she was looking for, and leave, this time for good.

Made wary by previous experience, Bethan approached the spot where she had stood tugging at Richard's hands. Breathing anxiously, she glanced down to where she calculated the boy had been standing when she tried to give him a helping hand.

The evidence of his struggle was there, sure enough, but that was all she could see. Nothing else. Just thick, peaty earth that had at least partially swallowed up and hidden a wartime bomber-plane for years.

Remembering that, despair filled her. How foolish she was, hoping to find something as tiny as a ring. Yet hope and determination couldn't be quite extinguished. She might be on a fool's errand, but she wouldn't give up without a try.

Bethan recalled how small objects dropped around the home often landed in unexpected places. A ring should be visible. It was light in weight, it was shining, and it shouldn't sink in. She lay down on the grass, craning over further than she would have done if she was standing on the edge.

After staring straight downwards, she let her eyes drift left and right. There it was. A tiny, shining circlet. It was further down than she had expected, but nevertheless she had been right. The ring had slipped off her finger when she had given Richard a hand-up.

She must get it, even though the thought filled her with doubts. She had been alarmed for Richard, who had been unaware of the danger. Well, he had got his trophy, and Bethan must emulate his success.

She stood up, staring around the site, to see if there was any easier way. But the ring wasn't near the bottom, or near the top. It had lodged itself awkwardly in a place to which she could only scramble down the loose earth.

She sat, her bottom on the grass, legs dangling over the edge. Care would be needed, if she wasn't going to cover the ring over with dislodged soil. Recalling how Richard had slid down on his behind, Bethan resolved to follow his example. Only she didn't want to slither to the bottom. She wanted to take it stage by stage.

Digging her heels into the soil below, she tried to make a platform landing-place where she could sit before she dug out the next ledge. Although her heart was pounding away in overdrive, it worked very well. Steadily she descended. Another two ledges and she would be there.

She made it. Alongside where she sat on the damp soil, it was possible to reach out and pick up the ring. Her fingers closed over the precious object. She let out a deep sigh of gratitude.

This time it would not go back on her finger, to risk losing it again because its size was wrong. When a jeweller had carried out the necessary craftsmanship, and made it fit her finger, then she would wear it.

Bethan's jeans had a pocket with a strong zip-fastener. Carefully, she slipped the ring in there. She still sat, bathed in a warm glow of satisfaction. She thought of Ray, and all he stood for, the fact that he had given her something precious. But the most precious thing he had given her was his love.

Minutes passed, and still Bethan did not move. Maybe the shock of finding out that the ring had gone, plus all the walking she had done today, had drained away her energy.

But she had to climb out of this place, and that would be even harder than what she had done before. Trying to gather her flagging energy and spirits, she gazed around, as Richard had done, trying to assess if there was any easier escape route. Richard had been right. This place was as good as any other.

The simple matter of turning round to start the climb made her heart thump unevenly.

Holding her breath, Bethan stood up. Seconds passed, then she turned, trembling with relief, as everything around her stayed exactly as it was. The footholds she had made on the way down faced her like a staircase. Somehow, the enormity of climbing back up there seemed greater than before.

Suddenly a picture flashed into her mind of the Bethan she had been; face impeccably made up, nails painted, dressed in a fashionable evening outfit. Now look at her, with muddy hands, soil-wet knees, tangled hair. The contrast was unbelievable. Twelve months ago, if someone had told her about this, she would have laughed in disbelief.

She laughed now, great bouts of mirth tearing at her, maybe relieving the tension, until, sharp as broken glass, she realised how foolish she was to make any unnecessary movement.

Laughter cut off, Bethan steadied herself, and managed the next step up. Then the next. This way, she told herself, I'm going to be all right. Take it one step at a time. Don't think about anything else.

Halfway up she paused, her lungs straining for relief. Standing shakily on her insecure perch, dizziness swept over her. Striving to fight off the blackness that threatened to engulf her, Bethan's hand groped out for something to hang on to. Soil crumbled and disintegrated at

159

her grasp.

I mustn't fall, said the voice of fear in her head. But her blind reaching out had caused the very effect she dreaded. A slow avalanche of soil began in a trickle beside her. Her bewildered eyes saw it change from a trickle to a stream, to a river. Panic still held in check threatened to break its bonds as she felt the ground tremble underneath her feet. No, she whimpered. No. Don't let it happen.

Even as the thought was formed, Bethan felt her foothold crumbling. Powerless in the face of relentless nature, she was carried downwards by an ugly mass of dislodged earth. The fall wasn't far, the soil was soft, but the stones bruised and cut her body as she lay, numbed with shock, at the bottom of the excavation.

She lay, an inert bundle of mud-sodden clothes, staring up at the sky, where the clouds were rippled in ridges, like the sand sometimes was on the seashore.

That's a mackerel sky, Bethan told herself. It usually means fine weather. Then mercifully the blackness closed in again, comforting, seductive, blotting out any need to think or worry. She fainted.

How long it was before she swam back to consciousness she didn't know, nor at this point did she care. A kind of numbness possessed her, removed her from the present scene and situation. Her mind wouldn't focus. She closed

160

her eyes against the glare of the light. For now, any other world outside this muddy chasm was suspended.

Time ceased to have any meaning, as though there was nothing at all beyond this place, this oneness with the earth on which she lay.

Maybe it will be my grave, like it was for the pilot of the plane, was her one blurred thought. She dozed, blotting it all out again, for it seemed too difficult even to shape thoughts, and string them together.

Bethan awoke with a jerk, shivering with cold. The sun was lower in the sky, and warmth had gone. How long she had been here she had no way of knowing, but a glance at her wrist-watch told her it was well into evening.

She struggled into a sitting position, brushing away earth from her hair and clothes. Surely someone would come and find her, although the only person who had seen her set off on this errand was the duty officer at Linwell Air Club. She hadn't told Ray, nor had she told Richard.

Would the duty officer attach much importance to the fact that he hadn't seen her return? Maybe he had gone off duty, and been replaced by someone else.

Bethan knew now that she couldn't get out of here without help, and the prospect of being alone in such a place at night filled her with dread.

She sat, arms around her hunched-up knees,

reflecting how foolish she had been, not telling Ray about it. Because by now, surely he would be wondering at her prolonged absence, and even if Richard had told him about their visit to the excavation site, what reason would Ray have to think that Bethan would go there again?

A feeling of utter helplessness engulfed her. She was here in this predicament because of her own foolishness, and for no other reason. Even when she had come to this place with Richard, there had been two of them, and one could have gone for help if it had been necessary.

Shouting for aid would be useless, because there would be no other person within miles. Shakily, Bethan got to her feet, brushing off what remained of the clinging soil. Had the airman been alive when his plane crashed here, or was he already dead?

She walked around, cautiously bringing the use back into her trembling legs. A nasty goblin of misgiving prodded into her mind the idea that it could be days before anyone came past this place. Maybe she should try again to scramble up those treacherous banks, but common sense told her that this would wear out what little strength she had.

Maybe it would come to that. Bethan's mind sheered away from such an eventuality.

It was colder now, and the light was beginning to go. Helplessly she looked around, wondering what shelter there was against the night, and there was none.

I chided Richard for wanting to come here, she thought. But I'm worse. Much worse.

She sat down again on a soft patch, where the stones were fewer. Time drifted. It could have been minutes, it could have been an hour, when her ears picked up the faint sound of voices.

Trembling all over, Bethan stood up. The voices sounded far away, but as she strained her ears her heart beat like a hammer in her head. With a great effort of will she tried to force herself to be calm.

Perhaps a minute dragged by, perhaps longer. She knew they were coming nearer, and please God they could only have one reason for heading this way.

It's too soon to shout, she told herself shakily. I must wait. Just wait.

It seemed an eternity; then she knew that these voices, strong, masculine voices, belonged to people who were heading this way.

'Here,' she croaked, in a voice that sounded strange and distorted. 'I'm down here.'

It's not loud enough, she told herself in desperation, then tried again, but it wasn't much better.

As she looked up, Ray's face peered down at her. Then two other faces, men she vaguely remembered from Linwell Air Club. Giddiness swept over her.

'Are you injured?' called Ray, forcing Bethan

to concentrate.

'No. Just frightened.'

'Don't be. We'll soon have you out.'

It was the same cheerful, steady voice that Bethan knew he would always use in a crisis. How have I been so lucky she asked herself, tears forcing themselves out of her eyes.

'We're going to pass down a rope, then another. Tie one firmly round you above the hips, and the other under your armpits. Understand?'

'Yes,' gasped Bethan. Her hands felt useless, but she managed to do it.

'It might hurt a bit,' warned Ray.

Anything, thought Bethan, anything to get out of here.

At the top she stood swaying, wondering why the world was spinning around. Silently, one of the Air Club men handed her a pocket-flask of brandy. It stung her throat, and made her cough, but the fire raced through her veins.

'Can you walk?' Ray asked doubtfully. She nodded. He doesn't waste words, Bethan told herself. Her legs were like jelly, but as the party went along they gained a little strength.

Back at the clubhouse, Ray said to her, 'You'd better not drive just now. Hop into my car.'

When they returned to Wood Hall, Mrs Challis had coffee and sandwiches waiting. Relief was written on her face. It all seemed so

164

peaceful and secure that Bethan burst into tears again.

'We'll take yours upstairs,' Ray said kindly. 'I think you've had enough for one day.'

'How did you know where I was?' she asked, horrified to see in the mirror her dirty face, where tears had formed runnels.

'Richard presented me with his trophy. He was full of it, and what you'd done today. The way that boy has come along is amazing.' He gave Bethan's shoulder an affectionate squeeze. 'He was so proud of getting out of that place, with only a hand-help from you. Then I remembered how uneasy you looked when I mentioned your ring. I knew you'd lost it.'

Bethan gave a wobbly smile. It was going to be difficult to keep any secrets from Ray.

'I checked at the Air Club,' he continued. 'The duty officer had written in his notes "Woman and boy walking to ruined plane. Returned. Then woman came back later alone".'

'Where are the boys?' asked Bethan, remembering the anguish when Tom had disappeared.

'I sent them to bed, but they're not asleep. Sleep is what you need now. I'll say goodnight.'

Bethan slipped out of her filthy clothes, then took a shower, which eased her aching body.

Ray hadn't mentioned the ring. All he had concerned himself with was her safety. The

165

door was open a crack, and she could hear Ray moving about downstairs. At the foot of the stairs he paused.

'Sweet dreams. And angels guard you.'

She knew, she just *knew*, that he only said that to those he dearly cherished, to the people he loved most. It enfolded her like a warm and comforting blanket as she drifted off to sleep.